The Ivory Hour

(A FUTURE MEMOIR)

LAYNIE BROWNE

SPUYTEN DUYVIL

New York City

Acknowledgements

Grateful acknowledgment to the editors of the following journal publications in which excerpts from this work originally appeared: *Exploring Fictions, Fifth Wednesday, New American Writing, Ocho, Typo, and Wig.*

Grateful acknowledgement to the editors of the following anthologies in which excerpts of this work originally appeared:

War & Peace 3/ The Future
edited by Judith Goldman and Leslie Scalapino, O Books

Wreckage of Reason: Anthology of Xxperimental Women Writers Writing in the 21st Century
edited by Nava Renek, Spuyten Duyvil

In memory of Stacy Doris

The Ivory Hour
(A Future Memoir)

"We must for dear life make our own counter-realities"
—*Henry James* from Letters

"What is the weight of light?"
—*Clarice Lispector* from *The Hour of The Star*

"Why should I abandon my ancient love
inherited from earlier births?"
—*Mira Bai*

Preface

Dear Text Travelers,

Speak to whoever you will

This book is unbound by time

Contents

Legend I.

Characters and their Derivations

GRAY = Graham Fielder + the light haired foreigner

HANS + all beardless boys

BEA = Macabea revised + all anonymous mothers + all torch carriers

ZURG = Zurg (though not recognizable to Buzz as Zurg) + Horton Vint's questionable side + Olympico revised

STARLA = Cissy Foy + Starla + all anti-heroines of ambiguous intent

BUZZ = Buzz Lightyear + Horton's noble side + Rosanna Gaw

MIRA = Mirabai + Miriam + all female prophets, saints, poets + all devotional song

Legend II.

Characters and Their Allegiances

Zurg > Zurg
Buzz > Gray
Starla > Zurg
Gray > ?
Bea   > her child(ren), all mothers
Mira > <

Legend III.

Key to interludes in the book, in which Henry James, Clarice Lispector, Mirabai, or Pixar characters make brief appearances within the text, or in which they have returned to rewrite particular sections.

HJ = Henry James
CL = Clarice Lispector
M = Mirabai
PC = Pixar characters

Legend IV.

Character Sources

from *The Ivory Tower* by Henry James
GRAHAM FIELDER, CISSY FOY, ROSANNA GAW, HORTON
VINT

from *The Hour of The Star* by Clarice Lispector
MACABEA, OLYMPICO

from the *Moomintroll* books by Tove Jansson
the INVISIBLE CHILD

from Pixar films and adaptations
BUZZ, ZURG, STARLA

Instructions for Latecomers

or

"When"
Is the reader:

A Time-Based
Interactive
Preface

(The Invisible Child Speaks)

1. Time is not innocent or separate. It is our inheritance.

2. Somewhere else is a perverse intersection which does not exist. You may swing your arms now, or not at all.

3. Who will speak this pre text? I am speaking because you don't know yet if you can trust me.

4. Where is the place where text ends and one begins?

5. What cannot be written is the reason you exist not only in text but in a body.

6. Characters speak across centuries/cultures. Texts converse. Comics/kids' art hurled into conversation with the dead. The sacred and the secular share a cup of tea.

7. The plight of the characters is that they are all in conversation with texts and not with persons.

8. This is also everybody's spiritual autobiography.

9. Text consumes something as it enters and later becomes what it dreams.

10. Dream is the other garment of time.

11. Letters, (or character) are also postures which—in various sequences—may send a message.

12. The weight of inheritance is in time and not in things. (Reformulate this statement to foreground the physical world).

13. We are all latecomers to the future.

Alternate Preface:
by The Invisible Child

Forgive me for beginning again. It is all I know how to do.

Please sign your name here. _____.
Then impress your desires upon the page in any language or century.

Please make room within this passage for any who might arrive. There is extra bedding in your ambient thought. I can see that you are tired. This is no surprise considering that you have been existing in a century of preludes akin to natural disaster. Recline here while you consider that this alternate entrance has been ascribed exactly for your comfort. Who can see a thing when one has become it?

Everything begins with your passage here. Without you it ceases to exist.

Like a child who believes her eyelashes will protect her from the dangers of looking directly into the sun I must admit something. I have been gazing directly at my undoing. Are you running across the surface? That is one way. Someone is speaking to you—sitting across from you at an intimate table.

Every such table in the world began with concentration. There must be the legged and the legless and the eight-legged horse of Thor. As you wish so you shall proceed. Over a cup or the back of any animal.

Send me your coordinates and I will coincide.

By whichever mode come inside this volume of possible undertakings and undertake something. Here is a glimpse at what you may find: scientists with missions and without. An Institute in the process of instituting something. Meta-amorous adventures. Re-incarnation. The cost of these draperies we call sky. Reasons for my invisibility. An inherent inheritance.

Book One:

Gray

(Children of Accident)

Buzz

PC:

Buzz purposefully sets out to work.

HJ:

It was but a question of leaving his own contract-ed vehicle, of landing upon unstable terrain, thus any terrain consisting of others and their insupportable unreliability, of crossing his own protective threshold to step out to the gate, which even with the deliberate step of a truly capable being he could reach in three or four minutes. So, making no other preparation than to lift his clear visor he made his way in heavy white boots with ample blinking gadgets attached to his person.

(end HJ)

While he walked he considered the health of the Institute, thus being his work, his unstable terrain, and the possibility that his project would be lost and again supplanted. His greatest ally, a virtual com-panion, was in the midst of completing crucial com-putations and would soon expire. And upon these computations would rely the weight of such an inheritance—he tried not to focus upon its weight. To whom would this project be given? And yet this was not all for his vision it seemed was unbound by finite forms, by reason. He was consumed with possibility, delighted by the prospect of what he had already intrinsically begun. All forms appeared to him possible. In his solitary state he also pondered one and another alliance which might make his future research possible. And while these concerns were true and pressing it was also true that his finer interest upon this particular day had to do with the imminent arrival of Gray. Nonetheless, appearing as usual in the midst of a quarrel between two co-workers, Buzz repeated his usual refrain: "I come in peace."

The common din of the place, metallic chatter, the unwashed windows and the slumped posture of postulates about their microscopes and computers seemed to inform him, however, that there had been as of yet no arrival.

His person therefore, not certain where to affix itself, bumbled amiably about for some time, literally bumping edges as he passed them. He landed upon a large stool and began speaking through various channels to his co-workers.

Mother of all cells.

Pass me some basic definitions please.

Biological repair system, status?

Theoretically, will divide without limit to replenish.

Did each daughter cell remain, or adopt a specialized role?

Controlling this differentiation process is—.

Excuse me?

Controlling this differentiation process is still—.

Is? Is it operable? *Now* is it?

Controlling this differentiation process is still—?

In question.

Buzz

All research is related to probing. To the absence of what is known. Following the curvature of a distant body. Untouched. I stood back and fell into reason. Reason and its relation to non-reason. Reality and its opposite. Both escorts wallowing accordingly at my sides. One with computation, the other pouring something into a glass and beckoning me to drink. Such charming assistants. Dare I say, I need no corporeal accompaniment? I am wrong and also blameless. I am worthy and without counsel. Please arrive and counsel me. You who think I am your counselor. The assumed is interchangeable with the unknown. And the unknown may become known as quickly as a person enters the room.

To make sense of the code of entanglements—genetically entrenched code which combs my speech, moving between embankments. The text of the code in which I live. So I laugh. Am I burdening you? I might ask when he arrives. With this coat of many converts. White coat, besmirched with investigations. Come, investigate me. Now I must sit down upon this pile of undesignated beakers. Break something which once was beholden.

Containing nothing. What is arrival? Doctors in Perth are embarking on new research to determine, as I pace my own resignation, early signs of cancer detected in a breath test. Funding, write a grant in my sleep? Another perch. Meanwhile, we fall behind if we do not pass additional legislation allowing somatic cell nuclear transfusion. Where are the benefits, Gray might ask? Have a seat and I will tell. Consider the benefits of deciphering the code in which you live. Determined in strings of letters.

To make sense of walking embattlements, passing obligatory mandates, exemplary research assistants, impeccable laboratory facilities. The safest and most up to date. Will none of this impel?

I will offer him a taste of what is at stake, the staggering list of proponents. The hidden history of the Institute which must not be hurried in confession.

Buzz

He took himself from the premises to walk. Along the way he would be wanted, with all of those assembled for a similar purpose.

He arrived beyond the morning after some confiding along the long lean strip of highway—far from his destination. To his own taciturn notebook he spoke, and the riveted oral recorder took this down, including all of the pauses and breaths he performed as he articulated his thought. Until his attention was broken by another, walking to recant or perhaps recoil a direction.

Hello. He looked up, unaccountably interrupted.

In an instant Zurg had assessed Buzz, looking down, distracted, unblinking and not exuding his usual assurance. He had the type of composure only possible for the self-contained innocent. Today he was deliberate. Speaking in low tones. And, given their history, Zurg was going to probe.

He fell into step. Borrowed his form audibly as he walked. Not asking anything first but simply observing.

The project?—he began.

Yes, the mother cells they are not yet, or—we are not yet certain of the daughters, of their whereabouts of their—how shall I put it, he wondered, and paused.

Of their choices.

Not the right question thought Zurg. Again silence. Walk back with me? We'll be expected shortly.

As they moved down the leaner strip of highway they soon entered the virtual countryside, or as it was now more often called the Future View. It began with a cunning dark lake upon which appeared small glossy boats and persons of all ages attired for summer. As they continued, the mock season changed to secure skaters and snow.

Will we ever, he asked.

Much better to look at—than what's beneath.

Yes, the veneer. His look dropped again.

Zurg was like Buzz in that he was replete with constant plans (though his differed in that one might call them campaigns rather than aspirations).

He said, Starla indicated she would have liked to join us but that she is held up at the Institute in preparations and she is wanting to hear from you. Especially about the arrival of your protégé. We're all very much looking forward to seeing him.

Without realizing that he had done so, Buzz stopped moving. How was it that all of these others had some claim, some opinion, some anticipation? The somewhat absurd arrow he stunningly felt was that he had no desire for Gray to meet all of these persons.

Zurg was noting Buzz's face, saying nothing at all. So this is the note, he thought.

I have just heard of it myself, and have not yet seen him.

Zurg smiled. Of course this morning he arrived at the transport. Starla would like him to dinner tonight. If you agree.

What particular interest does she take in him? He asked, somewhat stirred but still maintaining a forced semblance of his former containment.

Zurg replied, I believe at the Endocardium Station furthest quadrant abroad she met him—but then as I remember it, it wasn't him was it? She met some colleague or relation of his. She knows all about him through a correspondence with this friend, and he apparently has taken an interest—.

Gray—has taken an interest?

Starla herself will tell you all about this relation. That would be better I think. Zurg was quiet a moment and then continued, But I must confess I am no less interested in his arrival and the question of what part, if any, he will be given of the project.

Buzz stopped and stood gazing at the veneer. Obliging himself to speak.

He began hesitantly, I want to talk to you. There was a limp, or a lilt to this admission. They took seats upon a rock ledge at an overlook, spontaneously, as they had done so many times.

I'm not trustworthy, Zurg protested.

You must be. At this they both looked away from each other.

And then Zurg began bluntly, What did you do?

Nothing.

Which was?

Gray had a choice, he offered, gesturing at the ve-
neer. He paused and then continued, To leave.

Meaning?

I convinced him.

Convinced him, why?

To protect him. I had him written out of the pros-
pect.

And what is the story of this influence?

No different than the story of boys admiring boys.

Is that all?

Buzz did not reply.

What happened? The story?

Stories make the world, Buzz offered.

Yes, they do. And I'd like to hear this one. And not
so very abstractly.

Our families were friends. I was older. I *am* older.
Still.

And?

No preliminaries.

A unique friendship?

You could say that.

Your feelings were returned?

That is a question I could not entirely explore,
considering the circumstances.

Circumstances?

I was responsible—to help him.

As to what lies beneath the veneer.

In a way.

You had him written out and now you have once again interfered on his behalf?

I went to my mentor and encouraged him.

And therefore he may be better equipped than any to pick up where we have, shall we say, muddled?

Yes, he is uncontaminated by our view.

You mean our superficial false lookout, Zurg said, pointing to the distant lake.

My thoughts exactly. And I will call upon you to help me preserve his unusual vantage. We all will need to see as he sees.

And is the arrangement complete?

It soon will be. If Gray agrees.

Then what do you fear?

Buzz paused, knowing it would be difficult for Zurg to see. He answered calmly, as if in antidote to all he felt—.

My success.

Zurg

He came from the back, the outer portion of what would seem to be outer space to those who had seen him arrive, alien to the sun, with pasty skin and yards and yards of secondhand trench coat. Black sunglasses and hair stiff with gel. But he soon learned to wear a white t-shirt as well as anyone, to find more fashionable sunglasses at the drugstore and to choose the right hairdresser. All he had to do was find the man with a decent haircut himself. He could not have relied upon his own powers of description to imply the subtle shape suggested by his head, which was always a shade ahead of his body, poking ably, nimbly into crevices where he imagined might lie the greatest richness of information. How to become was what he coveted. And he eagerly though cynically read every pitch, every spam, every form, every notice which might lead him to the possibility of anything he did not currently possess. So, mistakenly he took to the dream of possessing all that there was to possess. Though he did notice this wasn't helping him, there was always the prospect of more, and the possibility that more would lead to more.

Starla

(Looking at photograph of Gray, on a computer screen).

Hair falling down upon his face. So this is what it looks like. Chosen for his eyes. Was that rude of me? He is a person and must look like something.

That is a lie. Honesty is something. But is it? Not more than you already have (let them down).

Why some meetings are so momentous and others so deflating—which will it be? He read from the oral recorder. One of those nether voices.

But in person this fair-haired foreigner will be _____?

Do I write in prose or allow myself to disintegrate into particles, obstacles, familiar beings, work to or therefore, folding fixatives—fall into a personality?

Did I do the right thing, involving a drink, my sleepy paramour, a grill, a youth, all day Future View gaming? Absence or doors closed, lights out listening to all of that noise instead of sleep. To be out in the night, in fog, it is cold, Why don't I have a view? When will I have my own speedway or room or time or even a body which moves freely despite expectations?

I'm still being considered. I'm looking at happiness. What does this mean? Difficult. I become swallowed. Perhaps I should work now, when there is time. I will order, erect and erase. They will build a dynasty of genes.

The lists are long and if you've ever left one environment for another, you might understand. In certain circumstances garments can shield me from my emotional setting. The inadequacy which really is not about the way you appear, the long arc in your nose, the sun-glorified skin. Your social manner being to retreat, to watch, to listen.

Gray

I am nowhere, and if I were to tell you the story I would tell you first plainly that location is not and has never been what it seems. We are ultimately fixed by other means regarding where we truly dwell. I am drawing near the influence of persons. Persons, not place, create residence.

The land resides in itself. And that is why it is such a comfort. It asks nothing of us. But that is the flaw of the century, in our thinking. Because nothing is asked does not mean nothing is required. But dare I speak in such a way to the persons whom I am soon to meet? I walk within the residing land. What is left of it.

What is left is the preoccupation with forms. The form of this body and what it will intrude or command. Before I enter how is my name carried? It is assumed by these persons that I am in some sense a child. Who ever heard of a speaking land?

I was sent away and then summoned. In the interim I have learned that in order to be effectual here I must learn another language. The name of the language I must learn has not yet been revealed to me. I am listening intently—trying to determine the language.

Much later I may learn that it is not a language of forms, or characters, but a language of listening.

Becoming is part of the premise which means nothing is complete. To be alive is to remain unfinished in a manner that seems both endless and minute. I will never get used to it. And at the same time I have surrendered in a curious fashion. I am an undone premise. This demands of me only persistence.

But how will I tell this to the unresponsive, the gadget happy, the drones and the ambitious, to those seeking only their own pleasure? Even those in the Institute obsessed with advancing civilization are missing something beneath the mechanism of movement. But I cannot expect anything to become clear before the eyes of the Institute immediately. I must walk and not calculate, listen and not insinuate.

Yes I have done so here, assumed unfairly and perhaps idiotically. I speak as if I know, when in fact I know only this place—its mark upon the skyline, sharp graphite rising—and angled. I know the reflective glass, in pictures. I know I was somehow carved here. There is a semblance of me. And though I have been absent, I have also been listening.

I know nothing about what occurs inside the building of reflective towers.

Being received by those both immediate and unknown is the predicament I find myself within.

Let me tell you where I have been. Sent off from a landscape of measurements into one of forging. There were no numbers, no hours, no chart upon the wall to mark my growth. No contained parameters. No scaffoldings from which to lean out and look down at an artificial garden.

I have been in a place which waters the night and calls day a rest. In the darkness I can remember the quietness, how shocking it seemed to me at first. And the land in its own design seemed initially untrustworthy. Remarkably independent, More so than any being I had ever met.

Mine is the story of a boy estranged from any sanctuary known as home, affinity. I was what you might call sent away from my identity. When my mother told me we were to leave there was an enviable corner in her eye—which I noted. This told me I could change things. It was her way of asking a question without admitting she was deferring to me. At twelve I knew this, but much more evidently, and I didn't know why. What was this other location and what had become of her once more determinate facial features? There was suddenly no protection from the land absence had determined. Suddenly, like departure, only we had yet to leave anywhere. My father leaving only his beautiful hands which I felt on occasion clasp my shoulders from behind. Did she know? I knew them at this threshold, his absent hands, urging me to investigate with the undertone and taste of question. What would I make of it, he seemed to ask. Or so I imagined. A boy of twelve in somewhat befuddled falling apart clothes. So I went where one is to go, hidden toward one's confidante. Away from the land of surface-seeming certainty and into the more fragrant regions of adolescent scribes who would know what wasn't spoken.

Spooked, he said, that was how I looked. We sat on the curb in the usual manner, knees visibly knocking together. Almost not touching at all. But certitude. Here. Buzz had absconded something from me. There is no future, he said. Now is where we are. So I questioned him. Must I go? This was partially a pleading for him to take me. Secretly or suddenly—away from the question entirely and into a region I only imagined as safe harbor. What did this antiquated phrase mean? I had read it in a book. About boats or boys, perhaps pirates. I didn't know. A boy of twelve with ghost hands upon my shoulders. A mother trembling of some indeterminate dis-ease which for lack of a better reason I ascribed to grief. What did I know, besides the curbside reverie, as a means to unburden my somewhat unbearable sense of self-enclosure?

Buzz didn't take me anywhere, exactly. He sent me. Was this betrayal? How could it have been when I'd never even asked what I had wondered. There were no words even, only an image of a boat. The missing physicality of terse engagements. The night which kept encircling something I couldn't have ignored any more than I could have described. But I knew at least that he inhabited, or had recently inhabited, such a question. The way he held his body and moved akin to some invisible current.

Safe harbor, safe harbor, but his eye loomed again. Preposterously, or disastrously, or anonymously. Nothing encircling the neck. No netting. This is where we are. Must I go? And even though I never uttered those exact words his gaze, which invariably tore through me, told me in no uncertain terms. There is no safe harbor. What you imagine is what you imagine.

Is it dangerous to imagine this? It is futile to imagine this. But relatively true if you are to leave.

He was basically saying, I am not that. I am not what you imagine. I am not your refuge, at least not of that sort. The grand entrance cannot be found in me. So, exit instead through this particular porthole. And go willingly, where she will take you.

There wasn't any "why" amid the interchange. "Why" interested me then as little as "no" and "later" and "you must." Because "why" existed in the same region as reams of books in which any point could be argued to infinity. I could have culled as many volumes of "why" on each side of the equation. But what I did not realize was that the "why" of the question was much more pertinent to understanding where I was soon to be, to become. There is no making up for age or blindness, which is just as well. So, seeing only what I was able to see, I went.

I dutifully followed my mother to that destination with no sense of "why" and stubbornly resisting any inclination to say goodbye. So, his eye loomed again and again from the safe distance of no curbs and no knees. And from this safe harbor, which I never knew myself to reside within, my questions began distractedly to walk.

And in the cities-systems I visited care was taken to shield me from anything reminiscent of the Institute. No uniforms or research laboratories. Instead, science infused with academic ethics. Think tanks alongside questions of what was deemed the flaw of the assumption of the "eternal atmosphere." We had seen it disappear, due to human idiocy. How to retrace and curtail further maiming of the first site? This against the backdrop of everything elsewhere, all rush and media. Medical thrusts brought to bear upon, first, regardless of the cost. The endless debates. And to escape and to examine these debates there were the usual cultural amusements to which I was drawn, objecting all along to the consumerist aspect of inhaling it all simply to say one had done so. That was the climate though, to say one had seen a show or heard a composition or been present for a performance. This was to replace possessions and even food. Persons, live transmission of works were to replace facts. Walking was to replace the sedatives once taken by my guardians. I recall a tangle of city nights unslept. Unredemptive atmospheres in cool colors, the length of various planetary days. Unblinking I resolved that neither one life nor the other could be called correct. The pursuit of earth science or the pursuit of the art of exile. Neither the land nor the person. Neither consumption nor non-consumption. Intoxication or sober awareness. I compiled my lists of opposites, choosing none of them.

In secret, I supposed I was alone in this occupation, except once. The moon was visible in our imaginations alone, though we insisted the sky had never been veiled and painted. I took out the memory only rarely. We walked to a place, a firepit constructed of stones we had found along the path. Of course this too was a prevarication, the real soil, actual original stones, had been replaced. In this spot the lists were burned. At least, metaphorically. In this spot many silent vows were made. I say vows because the unspoken knowing between various versions of myself comes into relief when I look back at these occasions somewhat piercingly. Secret volition. Paper to ash. And other things we were not to name or to know.

Starla & Gray

She enters the room and something is strained. Did he expect her to be so forthcoming in person? Not upon paper, but upon legs she entered. And then the thought passed. And they were standing in the noon light smiling. Pressed up awkwardly against the present.

You are my first escort, he said. The moment stretched and stretched again it seemed to him as he studied her and at the same time tried not to do so. She was taller than he had expected, and her presence seemed more commanding than he would have guessed.

Am I? she smiled.

After distant correspondence, to find an actual person. He found it a bit startling. And they were both aware, despite pleasant talk that the moment would allow little. His reasons for being present demanded a pace too rushed. At the same time he was recognizing a confidence in her tone that seemed to match her movements. They were both fluid and yet somehow abrupt. The glare of a posed hem, a sculpted inflection or sway which demanded attention. The thickness of her voice both direct, and supposing. And her eyes, less tentative.

I am to take you to the virtual companion, she ventured, and then to meet with you briefly afterwards.

I see, he answered falling into step.

And your journey was—?

Fine, uneventful.

And is there anything you need presently?

He walked head slightly down. Not certain how to reply. What sort of needs was she referring to? A map would be a help, he finally answered. They had come across the courtyard of the Institute and stood beside a black fountain trickling upon bright stone. Squinting in the sudden light.

A map. What sort of map? Of the local area? The Institute? she asked.

I meant a map of a different sort, he replied. And as she said nothing but continued to smile he added, Of the sort that will tell me a bit more why I am here.

If such a map existed I would certainly provide it for you—she paused, surprised. Now, she said, I'm afraid I must disappear and direct you to your meeting. I will see you afterward.

He nodded and headed up the walk.

Gray

His view was that he must make himself available to enter what had been chosen for him. He trusted this step back into allegiance with his past as easily as he had trusted his need for departure. And yet, he was ponderous now, in a room which would have been unimaginable for its elegance and usefulness, had he not found himself within it, left alone for a brief moment after such a meeting with the expiring virtual companion called M., who mysteriously seemed to draw all impressions of him as suitable within five minutes of making his acquaintance; and within such a brief interval had secured Gray's promise to step into the place which had been reserved for him all along, researching at the Institute, taking over a large parcel of the mission; and while all of this transition was being arranged, teaching for a spell, beginning immediately. All of this had occurred and he had as yet not even heard mention of, let alone seen Buzz, his one link. He told himself he was fine, though he was agitated enough so as to speak to himself, and found himself lifting levers, touching upholstery, reclining on the rich carpeting.

Starla & Buzz

She was on her way, having left him in the courtyard when her signaler called her to Buzz's station. He was perched upon a tall bench, as usual, examining his work in progress. The vials filled and refilled. Her eye greeted this array as she found him.

He heard her step and without even turning began, Starla. Thank you.

She stopped a few paces from him. Quietly waiting for him to complete his task. Whatever his task might be.

He finally turned, took off one glove, and then another. And how is all? he asked.

As planned, she replied, I have just delivered Gray to meet with M.

And how does he seem?

Well—though, she paused, considering how much to reveal. A bit confused as to what is expected of him.

I see, he said in a definite tone so as to give him time to take this in. So our Gray is a bit lost?

She nodded.

I must meet with him. Though a bit later. And I was wondering—he stopped again and held up one finger as a signal for her to wait. Then he turned his back to her and stepped to his screens and discs. He opened a locked cabinet with a key from his pocket.

She could not see what he was fumbling with inside. In a moment though, he turned to face her again and spoke. For the sake of confidentiality, I believe it would be wise if I were not the one to deliver him this information.

Buzz reached out and presented something to Starla.

She closed her hand around it and smiled. She asked nothing but merely stated, I shall go to him directly after his meeting with M. And with this she turned and was gone.

Gray & Starla

I have just come from them, said Starla.

From where, he asked, uncertain.

Oh, she stood dizzyingly still and he took in her intent.

I'm simply a messenger, she said, handing to him something.

A messenger?

From Buzz.

And this? he asked, with the small black card in his hand. Invisible when he closed his palm.

I don't know myself, she answered clear-eyed.

Should I open it now?

Should you?

Do you wish that I—

For me to say? I don't think I—

I see. Then I must find a place to contain things, at least for the moment. He turned his back and began to pace the room, as if searching for a sturdy structure.

It isn't actually—she stammered, took up the thread again, pausing.

Explain, please.

I can't exactly mark this out for you, but what I have given you is only one form of what you are to hold. It's only a metaphor for what you are really practicing by accepting—. Do you see?

You mean it's classified, my task?

Yes.

I must translate this, he asked, at the appropriate time?

Yes.

What if I'm not able to decode it?

You'll have to.

He was ready to ask further questions, to follow her clean, uncompromising expression. Yet she was already making the preliminary motions of exit. Eyes to the door. Person arranged. Exiting.

You'll have to, she repeated, and was gone.

He embeds the gift into his skin. Without having opened, examined.

He is the modern safe, code, computer—and somehow inviolable.

Starla

"Take her as an advertisement of all the latest knowledge of how to 'treat' every inch of the human surface and where to 'get' every scrap of the personal envelope, so far as she is enveloped, and she does achieve an effect sublime in itself and thereby absolute in a wavering world"

Henry James, *The Ivory Tower*

She wanders in thought to Gray, en route to the gathering where she hopes he will appear. Why will he never look up? Look up patch-faced, papier-mâché. In the academy he will not look up or across her routes. She covets not him but something containing him. What holds him intact, she wonders. What does he know? And this is easily confused with his person, his person being that which is easy to remember, and what is unknown being easy to forget. But she is dimly aware of the difference in this rare moment alone in her tin autocraft, restlessly spinning.

She crosses the night before, behind, crosses frosted legs (the light). The air-bridge at night when she cannot see the water is less frightening, unless she looks up to the cascade of lights to see the length of things before her. Who ever went to the old gamma quadrant, she wonders. The mutilated beverage sign reminds her to understand this setting. Unless she stalls. To think of fear or terror itself. Should she fly about, please everyone? It is easy for the mind to move rapidly in traffic. What the night is, potentially, seems more than you actually trace, she thinks. By movement. The desire to trace a star.

She wishes to retire to the star, to return, as if she were of the distant light. Who ever went beyond moving rapidly again, pushing her pedals, interrupting herself. And when she has arrived, she dabs the light from the mirror about her an octave high or low to pronounce herself ready. She uncrosses herself and admiringly steps out. Placing her steps within that very caliber which must be reminded of who she would like to become. The outline of the star still firm within her inner compass. Whoever is less frightening than him, she asks, considering Gray and where he will be apparently muddled. I could go, she thinks. He could enable me.

She hears another step behind her. It is the step of Zurg, unmistakably rushing to the same gathering. He, she considers, will always look up at me. He is tracing my outline in his thought. He could— and yet would he ever? Wishing to return again. But the light has caught his lapel and the sheen of his skin is a type of protection. And she will slow her steps. This isn't thought, she decides, it is inevitability.

Starla on Zurg

He was the sort that, when he was present he was so entirely present that she sometimes wished she did not exist, could not be seen and looked into, since when he existed for her it was impossible to look away. His sphere of influence rendered her speechless and made her feel that she had somehow lost all of her maturity and had been reduced to a pre-adolescent, one who couldn't drive a craft. One who had never yet known intimacy and thus existed alongside the questioning shadow. *Will it be you?* Once he wore a white shirt which seemed to scream. He came up to her and spoke some words, all of which were lost. She was simply thinking, how can you wear such a white shirt? And knowing it wasn't the shirt. Impossibly bright.

He would be on or he would be off. He would either look entirely past as if she did not exist or he would look so completely at her that she felt she had been undressed, not of garments but of any pretense of social poise. Any pose she had put on would be plummeted. She could not stand before him.

Once he simply touched her shoulder or her hair. She could not say what she had come to want to say. She could not look at him. It was that bad. Or that good. She didn't know.

But when he looked past so severely she did not

exist, like some simple lion raising a paw and continuing on, she did not dare interrupt his plan that she not exist. She simply ceased to exist. He had no awareness that he was doing this of course, but she learned in time that she was not the only one held and then dropped for long distances of silence. During these silences she spoke to herself incessantly. She pleaded for the rearrangement of her thoughts. She vanished and she uncompromisingly promised herself she would no longer be held under his sway.

Starla & Zurg

CL: In this increment one mustn't wonder who one becomes while residing within the heart of another. The heart of another is also your own. Therefore, to question this action is to question your own intention. That they had met here accidentally is not accidental.

HJ: She had been sitting in the forgotten spot, though perfect for such a meeting when he came shuffling past, looking out at the horizon until he nearly walked into her, sitting silently at his knee. She was dressed in several veils of white, which added to the effect of the landscape, and seemed both to envelop her and draw the eye. Has she become her surroundings so easily, he wondered? But then he brushed the thought aside, and he smiled and she in answer did so as well. And they sat down, sheltered by a rock overhang overlooking the shore, clasping hands as they did so, though only for a moment, certain in the sense that they might not be seen. Before they said anything at all they sat in silence, until she mentioned that she had just come from Gray. He gazed at her pointedly, but before he spoke, this expression conveyed his thoughts, though she knew that he could only have done so by the fact of her concentration upon him. And here she replied, internally, by looking down, that of course she would do her best to comply.

You see we both found ourselves with nothing, at twenty, he began, looking out ahead of him, and therefore we had everything in common. Except that he, with nothing, was completely unbound. He could make anything of it. He walked across town if he had no token to fly. And I myself would not even fly with a token. I would have required my own craft and my own pilot as well, were I to turn up.

So, he desired not to arrive in a particular style, but to arrive?

I could not surmount my own need but I could admire his lack. His showing up and taking pleasure in a virtual book. He didn't care to own anything. But he knew. Whatever it was. He could clothe himself in philosophy. He could cook with only a formula.

And you preferred to starve?

Rather than eat an equation? I couldn't help but to like him, to admire him for being what I was not. And now I'm afraid of what might become of him when he inherits all of this information, this wealth of—.

Of what?

Dare I say position? Or the inevitability of becoming one of us?

No, you shan't say it, she shivered. And he moved closer under the rock, and took her fingers again.

And you are thinking of all you have heard of him from your magnificent friend?

Not from my magnificent friend, but magnificently of him.

Ah, a difference.

I don't believe it possible that such a dear man could have spoken with such admiration about him were he not—.

Were he not?

Were it not so.

Yes and your friend would know this out upon his genetic farm, riding the newest variation between horse and gibbon.

You are not to confuse his name, and you are to know that I have fallen so completely in love with my friend that I shan't ever feel the same about you, nor even does Gray have a chance of my falling for him, though even you, and all the rest of us may desire it.

Yes, good old man, the age of your grandfather? Such a dear old thing. He does spoil it for us all. Although his being dead does place a damper—

None at all, she said with a serious expression.

Was it his jealousy, or her own at work here, he wondered, again pressing close, not however free of the ghost just as yet. He said, I would hate to see all of this information perplex him.

And I would hate to see it not perplex him. That would suggest that he had already succumbed—. Here she faltered, but then retrained her thought to continue. That would suggest that he had swallowed without any qualms, that owning something is to know it.

I have no doubt that your charms are already at work.

Even knowing we have just barely met?

Yes.

Still—.

Still?

I would suggest that you be certain as you proceed that you consider the plan and—.

And not in hopes of inheriting myself?

My dear, he said let us be honest here.

Here, and not elsewhere? she laughed weakly. Anticipating his next move. So deftly he had wrapped his arm about her. How quickly she responded against her own will.

He will love you. If he does not already.

Why do you say this? she looked away.

Don't joke, he said leaning his head against hers a bit, fingering the fringe upon the edge of her wrap. We need not speak of it. It has already begun.

Who Are You Going = is Saying
(Starla & Zurg: A Play)

Carefully hammer solitude apart with such fists.
Beauty insists it is a rake hitting me upon the head. I
want to be generous. And I am not. With my time.
Whose is it anyway? Who said it was *your* time?
You are doing a very poor job of protecting me. Here,
sit upon this. It is just that when in someone's pres-
ence I don't even want to lift. (hangs her head)
You don't even want to lift?
No. Not even to have a face. If it could be seen.
Isn't that othering?
Despite what you think. I will come if I must. But I
will not show up. (Lifts her coat up over her face).
That person only admires you.
But that person mistakes me for "I".
Meaning herself?
Exactly.
You could come along without any face.
Undressed?
Well—.
I thought so.
What is so difficult about being present in the pres-
ence of—.

Dread? If you knew something I could tell you something else.

Oh?

If you knew something—.

I know something.

Such as?

I know something.

Such as why is it so difficult to be in the presence of (lifts coat over her face).

It isn't who you think.

Who?

My dread.

Who?

Mine is dreadless.

You mean you don't have any? You can just walk out into—?

I want to do that. (Gets up and walks repeatedly across the room).

That's only because you don't have a coat (laughing).

You would, wouldn't you (still walking).

Well, it's cold (draws coat around herself, changes positions).

Oh? Where is it cold?

Inside the coat, of course. Inside the dread, which you apparently don't have.

I do. I know something about dread.

Such as.

If I had it would look like this. (He draws a square on a screen). If I had it.

But because I don't I have only this (makes a hand gesture).

That doesn't count. If you knew something.

I know that I dread not having the dread. I know how to count your coats. And the number of times you've said you wouldn't show up.

Why would you want it?

What?

Any of it? (she gestures to her coat and her fallen head).

Because then I could walk away from something. As it is I'm always inside this container (points to his head).

Oh. Well, I have one too you know. It isn't any different in my case. In my case (gets up and starts opening and closing cases) I have various choices of where I don't want to show up.

In my case I don't.

You wouldn't.

What do you mean?

I mean that in order to walk away from someone first you have to walk toward them. (Both walk back and forth across the stage in mock line dance).

This is and it isn't what you came for. (Gets up and takes something from his pocket, a piece of paper).

Quite right.

You are and you are not what I desire.

If I could help it——.

You will and you will not leave me alone. Will you?

(urgently, grabbing his shoulders).

If I may interrupt.

Who? Who will you interrupt?

Mayfly don't bother me (moves away).

But who did you interrupt?

You mean, which one of you?

Hmm (crosses to a corner of the room, crouches down and hides in coat). What I mean is: see this? (Waves her hands in front of her). Can you see it?

No (looking confused).

Of course you don't. It is all passing. And we don't see it do we?

Is it my fault?

I certainly hope not.

Well I couldn't claim responsibility for that.

Which one of you? One of you might stand up at least. And say something (frustrated, impatient).

Which one then?

Isn't it obvious. The one who is responsible. For this (waves hands in front of her).

(He sits down, scratching his head. She moans audibly.)

Alright (she stands, takes off her coat) clearly I'll have to be the one to mention things.

Clearly.

This isn't what I came for.

What did you come for?

That isn't an answerable question. Would you care to rephrase it? Or maybe there isn't time for religion. In this case.

Nor for philosophy.

Not at all.

What about comic books?

OK. (Eagerly, they sit together on a curb and begin to read silently and to laugh. After a minute he stands up anxiously and says)

This isn't what I came for.

No (she stands).

Zurg

You pull an appositive from a relational spur

What you read is what you become

I am within the reclining action which speaks

Perhaps thought and therefore recycling sound

Subterranean specious the way she stood in the
Institute

Looking years lighter, diametrically fraught

No longer raven but spurious action or acclaim

Punctuation required of me is unknown

To recline as an action is sodden and incomplete

An active activate retrofitting device carries the
future sun

I imagine it will be all dresses

Despite your electronic and virtual bliss

Brushing up against elastic counter spiked

Recalcitrant stalkers up late and clearly

That I do not know the directional status of this
discourse

Is exactly the reason for its existence

Deliberate, the answer may not be yours or mine

Why is it so easy to go where we are not bidden

Upon a blue floor to move not all beautifully

We are no still life and what can be learned from a
fixture

Matches my own opposable promise

Buzz

(recounts a dream)

Substantially a dream we wish to cling to and not to forgo, forget, forge within incendiary mechanisms therefore go less childish wish—

From memory. I am invisible. There is a boy, in an old buttoned coat, secondhand military, or of some mysterious empire. Do we speak the same language?

Another language, instant kinship, affinity.

Is his name Gray? Is he from the destroyed cities?

We are in an abandoned castle, ruination. Cold and hungry. He must be saved from something. Unbathed. No matter. Longing is childish and innocent.

When I awakened I was lying in bed trying to retain the apparition. So pure in insisting upon merely presence and nothing else. Stirrings uncolored by adult consciousness. Complete belonging.

Clasping his hand in greeting or recognition. This has nothing to do with possession, as it wouldn't occur to us that other worlds could interrupt, interject.

Running down a hall where we were vaguely aware we should not have been at all. Damp grey stone. Where are we? Whose form is asking? Propelled down another tunnel and another.

Covering the same ground again and again. The expression on his face saves me. The difference between falling and falling has everything to do with the scaffoldings we construct. Finally he reveals to me why we have run to this dark passage.

Colin wanted to meet you, he says.

Where are we?

Colin, he points.

Who?

He points to a small stained glass window, visible only through a window across a locked courtyard. The head of a small bird etched in the glass.

O, I say, examining the bird. He must be a friend.

When I try to take the dream memory further, there is no crossing. No bordered kiss, no reclining embrace—in the original.

He has been deprived of companionship. As if crossing a sea, continually; there are certain ports at which he is able to stop. Colin is a port. There are other points in crossing where he cannot bid his mind still enough to enter.

It is a great mark of his confidence that he has introduced me

The glass bird stares and says nothing

We skip contentedly down the dark damp hall again and out into the light

You can live here, I say, because you are invisible

Gray & Buzz

"That concentrated passage between the two men while the author of their situation was still unburied would of course always hover to memory's eye like a votive object in the rich gloom of a chapel; but it was now disconnected, attached to its hook once for all, its whole meaning converted with such small delay into working, playing force and multiplied tasteable fruit."

Henry James, *The Ivory Tower*

PC: They finally meet, carrying lasers, blasting light everywhere and yet unable to find the missing treasure.

CL: And where were the bodies residing while the minds resided in a happily lost chapter, when once these two had concentrated until light could not contain them.

M: "Come and grant me Thy sight."

Gray startled, walking towards the room and suddenly the meeting which he had approached mentally through these many years of distance. It was now looming up within his physical reality. It wasn't a poor feeling and yet it surprised him, how he thought he was about to be disappointed. Not disappointed in Buzz, but those memories were about to be replaced with something pressing and vivid. He would be breathing. Buzz, who represented something, what did he represent? He perhaps might think of him as a part of his invisible anatomy. And what words would be spoken between them. Words then being completely insufficient and ordinary. There was nothing ordinary about Buzz. About their relation. So how is one to say "hello" and all of the preliminaries as persons do when they meet and meet often? To remember that Buzz was in fact a person, did in fact breathe, would have other society and friends, was to remember the unpredictable nature of persons as opposed to ideas. His idea seemed somehow safer. And yet as the moment approached he noticed his step increased. His breath became erratic. This, all of this, he said to himself clenching one slightly damp hand. He nearly tripped. And then the other thinking mind came into being, the one less young and more concerned with composure. How can I possibly represent anything useful now? I too must represent something, mustn't I, to him? Or is it possible that all of this is not reciprocated? That it is only I carrying the weight and lightness of our history.

And then more seemingly quickly than his thoughts reached any pliable conclusion, as they had not, his feet had carried him to the dwelling place. He had been escorted into one chamber and then another and taking all of this in visually, and before his mind had recourse to continue its wanderings, Buzz entered.

For a moment they stood and said nothing. This was not an ordinary moment. It was a moment which seemed to contain endless moments and endless re-adjustments of history. Had they both aged? Was it possible time had been passing? Yes. Both were detectible in the faces of their other. My other face, Gray thought mildly. He seems much larger, and blinking and not contained. He is smiling. I believe he is smiling at me.

They embraced. What could be said so such silence was broken? Gray wondered as he stood another moment breathing audibly thinking this must be yet another moment which becomes as a century. They were wise enough both not to speak but to suspend this time to take in the presence of the other.

And in the moments that followed, they spoke of when Gray had arrived, and his journey and the polite preliminaries as if ushering themselves through a necessary passage and into a brighter corridor where they then could resume their concentrated acquaintance. Concentrated by the passage of years. There was no mention of, at first, the reason for Gray's arrival, no mention of what was at stake for either.

Buzz too was surprised at what he saw. Would he have known Gray in passing? Gray who had been nearly a boy, barely grown and how he now possessed himself. Grown so much of this quality which he had once glimpsed in infancy a purity or shall we say a hypothesis of hopefulness, a promise. What I might have been, but was not. This was all still present, yet wordlessly Buzz could see how this quality had grown to assume the shape of the person in which it was once merely a glowing supposition behind the very young eyes. Still the eyes were young, but young in a second sense of knowing. And still the hands were fine and the expressions subtle but definite. And beneath all of this, the fringe of fallen hair, the wide shoulders strengthened, beneath the frame of the man resided this innocence which Buzz had so admired. He did not see it at first, as he was so taken with all else that had matured, but in conversation it did emerge, and Buzz was glad to recognize in such a short passage that what he had known remained. That he had, he hoped, made another correct decision in drawing him back.

Buzz & Gray

Buzz was gazing at him, not quite aware of the effect of his towering presence. His enthusiasm not masked by the blinking gadgets, the forthright correct posture. The flush of his face as he spoke seemed to flood—and Gray transfixed by this so long imagined figure now suddenly animated, speeding, as if the gap in their meetings had not occurred. Things are arranged, he thinks, not quite understanding but then remembering the virtual companion. His brusque questions. Another concentrated gaze. It seemed to Gray that since his arrival he had been transferred from one concentrated gaze to the next, and never for very long under the eye of one. The motion spurred him.

You did receive it? You did safely embed the information?

Yes, from Starla.

Then it is done. I'm relieved to hear this as you may have guessed we've had concerns about security. And that's why the indirect missive. I hope you don't mind.

No, not at all. Gray took this in. He hadn't recalled where he was, what was potentially at stake. He continued, and your virtual companion, M., is ill?

He needed to see you, to know.

To know?

Your sense allows him to expire.

This seemed odd to Gray, who found himself in a state of sudden dread. He asked, Do you mean to say I have somehow . . . hastened his passing?

You are enabling a change. He isn't dying of anything other than the weight of this inheritance. We've all adopted the coming transition.

Have I then too? I'm not certain that I understand. Or what I have accepted by coming. And should I begin to absorb the information? he replied.

You can do so as you wish or not. The main thing is, the transfer has occurred securely. It will take you some time to open and decode, which I suggest you do only in privacy and with adequate time. But you needn't hurry. The process has already begun involuntarily.

What do you mean involuntarily? Gray had no context for this explanation. And yet he intuitively knew something had happened since yesterday. It wasn't a conscious perception but something nearer to a buried insight.

Buzz was silent a moment, considering his friend. He walked across the room and offered him a beverage. Would you like to sit here? he asked, pointing across the room to a certain eminent seeming chair.

Gray said nothing but rose, taking the drink in hand, crossing to sit, all the while thinking, I do wholly trust this man, since otherwise I would not be here at all, let alone taking direction about what to drink, where to sit. There was something oddly comforting in the act of being directed. Something foreign to his recent adult life. Familiar in the history of their relations.

Buzz continued, There will come a time when all of the information will be forthcoming.

From you? Gray hopefully asked.

From your own self.

Gray again looked blank. He looked as if his eyes might have grown larger. As if they might in fact swallow him.

Buzz could not respond to this as well as he might have liked, but went on, the information will take effect. You have embedded it. It contains its own intelligence. Do you see?

Not at all, he answered bluntly, somewhat embarrassed, though determined to learn all he could and feeling certain that Buzz was, for the moment, the only one to whom he could reveal the depth of his ignorance.

It isn't immediate, he said, pausing to study Gray's reaction. And then continued, once this process becomes evident you will know when the task of consciously sorting the material will be appropriate.

This seemed to calm Gray a bit. He asked, And for the moment my task is?

There is immediate work to be done. Certainly. In fact, there is a class which has been on hold and interrupted, and I'm wondering whether you would mind taking it up. This was a cautious statement as Buzz was not at all certain how Gray would take to it.

Yes, of course, he answered, Your virtual companion did mention it. I'd be relieved to begin with some teaching. And it will take some time to set up my equipment and my lab space, for everything to arrive.

I'm glad, Buzz answered. And for a moment they were silent both somewhat relieved that they had gotten this far, that they had survived the weight of first meeting. That some understanding had been made. It was a perfect moment of silence perhaps, until it was interrupted by a messenger tapping somewhat aggressively and suddenly at the door. Buzz crossed to open, and there before him was the missive.

What is it, asked Gray, already trying to read Buzz's expression.

My companion, he nodded in Gray's direction though not fully looking up. He's worsened and I must go to him immediately. You will forgive me?

Book Two:

Mira

(The Motionless Realm)

"Writing is thinking."
Bhanu Kapil

"I craved a Ganges of words; how terrible these
tresses are, whose sole clasp is my hand and sole
emblem, the wind! It's like waking from a dream,
of the body, of words"
Chus Pato

Mira

Dear Advisor

You are never the same twice, and always the same. It is only the little "i" which unaccountably shifts. And the larger "you" to which I pivot hopefully. I have arrived in this body, adorned with such a world, completely insupportable, it seems.

Advisor:

It is only circumstances which change and you can be within them any noun, any verb, any adornment you wish. You are here now, in this personal garden.

Mira:

I see only asphalt, and cynics who do not depart from books.

Mira's Notebook

1. Nature is not a place. You are and you are not the lonely tree upon the hill.

2. Must you read with that pathetic inclination?

3. If you write the poem of what has happened, where is the happening of the poem?

4. If you write to display what you know, what do you learn?

5. Write what you know (not). Write the unknown.

6. Does your text dictate? Does your text listen?

7. An ant is crawling across my page and—

8. There is no window in the room.

9. Can you hear another voice besides your own?

Mira
in the Academy of Scowling

Please read from the middle—and then the broken—
we will only speak in—what do you believe in—
could not see the trees—walking with me this way,
to class—Mira, in conversation with her conductor.

Mira on the steps, carrying books, all of which be-
wilder her, then sitting among apparently fellow hu-
mans, but they seem not to look up, or out or into
each other's faces in a way which is not more than
preliminary. They all look back to their books, their
own writings, their own speech. Scowling. The Acad-
emy of Scowling. This seems to be the appropriate
measure then.

Mira looks up from her book. To ask: What do you
believe then is worthy of verse? Is there anything that
is not? The question is pointed upon her. She looks
at her classmates, not as if to say, *I am really looking
back upon my own skull.* She sees them, apparently
not listening to the silence she commands.

But I thought you were invisible, their anxious looks
seem to say.

You are uncomfortable with silence? she asks, or does she state this, avidly attaching her eyes to those of her onlookers.

From this moment something has changed within the space in the room. She finally responds, nothing is not worthy of verse, though that isn't as simple as it seems, since you'll have to make it so, not simply receive the statement—.

A question of leaving her own contracted plan, of leaving one classroom for another. With the deliberate step of truly massive intent she could arrive in three or four steps. She had heard the lecturer through the wall. She had listened.

Now she recounts to herself all that has gone badly in poetry class.

It was the wrong class, she thinks. And as she enters the second room it is as if the hour has shifted, and begun again. Instead of the poem built in structures of words, columns of unmasked words, as if, she thinks, one had been trying to insert every word in the English language into one's possessional page, here were organic structures already perfect in form, making up the cells and composing the skin of the tissue upon the hands which, next door, wrote the flawed verses of youth (for which Mira had little patience). They all want the life I have revoked for centuries, she thinks. They want no wandering amid uncertain rooms. They want the given. She studied the overhead projection, and concluded: biology.

Dear Advisor,

Do you imagine a saint would not be impatient? I am in human form again. I have a task. And until I approach that task, I may not begin. I may not begin in the wrong room. So, though it seems a poet might remain among poets, now a poet must move.

Mira looked up and Gray saw her visibly awake, taking all of this in. The rest of the class, though mentally present seemed somehow suddenly mechanistic, automaton-like, methodical-eyed in comparison. He could see this in the questions she asked saying nothing. And how did she come to be here? And did they fall into step as if this had always happened? This isn't what you are thinking, he thought, to the distant reader or observer of his circumstance, always living twice. There is something besides chemical, something besides molecule. We wouldn't need bodies to talk. He said this later to his oral recorder: *it is only that I would hate more than anything in this instance to be misunderstood.*

Gray digresses, *what do I mean when I say she is awake? Of course she is awake. Aren't all of my students awake? I don't mean that literally. What I mean is that there is an activity in her consciousness which is awake beyond simple wakefulness. Dear oral recorder, what do I mean by this? I do not know. I fear that I fall into the category of literally awake myself. She is awake on another register. Shall I call it a plane? I have no language to explain.*

Conversation day one:

You aren't on the class roster.
No I am not.

Why are you in my class?
I am a poet in the wrong room. So sorry. I shan't
come again, if this bothers you.
No it doesn't.

And your name?
Mira.

PC : She is the alien character everyone misunderstands and wants to be rid of in all of the James novels. She is not contained, not of proper parentage, broke.

CL: And so thinking, Mira enters the text as easily as she enters any reality. Not by thinking, but by becoming present beyond any notion of tense. Anyone who tries to explain this will fail.

HJ: With a complex diplomacy I object to the notion of these characters not being wanted by design. Of course they are exposed on every side, wanted by the reader and even by those weak-minded selfish and cowardly characters who think all is lost. The word "want" is simply too one-dimensional here. I shan't try to replace it, as that is perhaps another novel entirely.

Mira:

Dear Advisor:

Let me speak as if I were not any one character
Dropped from the nib
Time is flawed to enter.
You have no word for s-k-y
I'm imagining this. Do you mind?
The word has been erased
And yet I look up
Why have I been propelled here
with knowledge of my former births?
It is no longer 1498 C.E. There is no Rathor, no
Merta.
Which small fortress city, which palace must I flee?

Mira & Gray

He begins, if there's a person in the world who I
don't call a facade—!

It is as if you were now entangled.

You mean that when I *have* read or absorbed it I may
still not regret this embedding?

Mira mumbles (to herself)—take him from water
and he immediately dies.

Acquisition . . . by itself promises me information.

She is walking the woods and lanes.

Who is walking the woods and lanes?

Whatever you clothe me in I wear.

Mira

What shall I say when he asks? Occupation: saint, poet, mystic?

And furthermore nudge glistened real-doom. Reverse insistence. Scintillation. What is written. What is not. Of obstacles hidden. There is my body, wearied. The recipes, marred: "Ignore the limps. They will take care of themselves." Do not ignore that I am waiting for nothingness. To continue. I keep losing my place within what I am to become.

Half laughing he asks me: What do you mean you've *come back*?

Come back, did I say come back? I stare over my shoulder inquisitively, as if I could ask a former self. Shall I say 16th century, near Mertha?

From where? To whom are you speaking, he asks. Who is it you are writing to, endlessly, in that notebook?

Accusingly, the notebook. As if I had lavished its pages. Given what I have withheld elsewhere only between the indistinct covers.

Knowing I won't be believed, what am I to say to him? Am I distracting you (with my persistent supplications)? Do you want to sit down? On the floor? Here is a pillow. No, you wouldn't know my hometown.

He wants to know to whom I am writing. You, beloved, who I speak of, seem completely hidden here, in this century.

Here, where books are thrown away, written over. Milk poured out. Bounty and abundance upon each corner. And those sitting beside the shops, gutterless, hands open, are also mostly unseen.

Motorcars are the incarnation of what?

Of burning from interior caverns of the earth. Running dry. Moving quickly along stiff streets. Plank-like. Cities forewarn their inhabitants. Animals are kept separate. Fields and forests are for the fortunate. Where are the urban birds to provide song?

When I speak your name no one trembles or objects. They simply look at me blankly. As if I'd gone mad. This is implausible, more so than I ever considered. Exist within the invisible universe, where light is constructed only through inverse prisms. Filtered into the eyes of the unbelieving without their acquiescence. You enter.

I see the light enter their eyes. No gratefulness. Is there a remedy? Dear Advisor, this term, "advisor" seems less frightening to others. You and your many names. Please speak to me.

Who I am is always the catch. The circumference. You can't insist upon knowing such things. You come back. This I have learned. Seize what is given, even when it appears you are instructed in nonsense. My actions must amplify your meaning. I am charting the fluctuations of your breath.

He doesn't know does he? Such occupations are embedded before they may be chosen.

Mira & Gray

When X forbade creation of the new embryonic.
He softened the hit by—.
Promising some older preparations could still be—.
Denying the new embryonic.
Only 22 of the sanctioned cell lines have survived.
The lines are supposed to be immortal.
Were supposed to be—
And others, which survive cannot produce.
And others which remain are contaminated.
Grown on beds of mouse.
Grown on beds of?
Yes, this is no longer necessary. Still.
Can these be used for human—?
Xenotransplantation?
If pig heart valves—.
Baboon-to-human bone marrow transplant.
Have been approved.

Mira:

Come, beloved embryonic
quench my pain
The only immortality
is xenotransplantation
Who will listen to me?

Stop, Mira, this is—.
Not what you expected of me?
I don't know
Let me tell you then.
You?
Use me. I am of course ill.

The words echo in his head. *Use me, I am of course ill*. Ill? Why didn't you tell me? He looks away, away past the initial meeting in his classroom, the studied lines of poems. The uncertainty. Why is this? And where? He summons his gaze. Brings it back to her face. Ashamed, for not noticing what she most certainly must have considered from the beginning. The beginning of what? And now this unexpected offering. He is confused, as if some great misfortune has befallen him. Though he is not at all convinced.

She meets his gaze with no hesitation. Her eyes are full, and yet, there is no attempt to shield herself from being seen. Her face is as transparent and open as if she were speaking of nothing.

If I cannot be of use, she pauses to think how to say what is to her so simple, so unnecessary to explain, and yet, knowing he doesn't at all see it yet. If I cannot be of service I must certainly fail.

CL: Until this moment it has been unclear to Mira why she has entered the story at all. What must a poet do? What is inferred by another? Embodiment?

Mira & Gray

You want a transactional verse? Mira asks.

What do you mean?

You wish to be told what will make you apparently real, or apparently a success, in the world of—.

Well, certainly in the world of—.

How could I possibly tell you?

Reading poems while they watch her blood spin up from the tube in one arm, and over her head spinning, spinning and back down into the other.

Because you have arrived yourself.

I have arrived only within my own form, not within yours. Tell me, what runs through the woods without making a sound, without moving at all?

Where do you find such. . .

Probing questions—.

Yes.

In a child's magazine.

I don't believe you.

It was a riddle.

You are incomparable. Will you tell me now?

Tell you what?

The answer.

To which question?

To the riddle, first.

What runs through the woods without making a

sound?

And without moving at all. Are you ready?

Yes.

Am I remiss? Perhaps the research goes nowhere. Are my cells poetical enough?

He doesn't answer. But looks up again to the tube in one arm, spinning, spinning up over her head. Now are you trying to speak to the first question as well? You haven't answered.

How can I possibly speak of your path.

I see.

Sight is the least reliable of the senses.

Why is that?

Because you can only see what is near, to begin.

Perhaps—and listening?

You must learn to somehow rely upon silence.

That is your advice?

If you don't listen to silence it sounds all the same. There is no learning from it.

He pauses, and then begins, Yes. It is almost finished now Mira. He removes the needles. So small they can barely be seen.

She sits up, slowly. And you are, if anything, distinguishable. The problem is everyone in this world now seems to be bent upon becoming distinguishably absent.

Why do you say in *this* world?

I should say, in this *time*.

Has time changed consciousness so much?

Yes, and is it possible that time will continue to do so? And how might you contribute to that?

This is more difficult than—.

What, than simply to write? She pulls her sleeves back down to her wrists, and rises.

Mira

Inside or outside of certain light.

I am standing beside the circle made by someone's skirt.

Thus being within and outside.

Who is wearing this light is who is leisurely waiting

or linking—thought is a parameter for premonition.

You are conveniently inside of my light. Therefore is it necessity which seeks you more than any self seeks a presence.

So stepping toward you. Through this light I am sewn.

Upon your premonition I appear.

Within your word I am made.

Here I will allow myself to fall.

Mira In-verse

A head tilts in front of her and she cannot see the face of the reader. She tilts her head and remembers the woman behind her, who will in turn tilt her head in the opposite direction (with a scowl which she perceives through the back of her skull). This person unseen behind her hasn't yet learned to enjoy the depth of the room—depth of other bodies—.

She tilts her head again at an angle so as to see. Mira thinks, *If we aren't going together, we aren't going. Does she know? The reader, so scholarly, and this woman beside my friend looks from the side like someone I know, with dark dyed hair falling. Tissue thin beige upon whose sheathe matching skin. She is not at all as I remember, the reader. Filmy, between the bare shoulder blades, deliberate gold.*

Somehow the entire evening is this, a head tilts in front of her. She must coax herself to enter. Mira tilts her head into sound. Dark-dyed language circling the perimeter of—not at all as she remembers.

Coax attention back toward inscribing the text. *Will I be able to remember?* The thought disrobes, the page is opaque with listening. The sound is the subtle carriage in which we become meaning. The poem is the arc of occurring as one listens, each time actualizing. It isn't what the head tilting expects. The head tilting is a resonance which shifts.

Coax. Oneself again to enter. *Tonight it will be difficult or it will be effortless.* To speak to each person upon every side. Just as, *if we aren't going together, we aren't going* doesn't refer only to the cafe, afterward.

Mira & Gray

How was the event, he asked, as he swabbed her arm with cotton and alcohol.

Socially challenged.

How so?

Like a six-year-old child, who asks his friend to the playground without looking at her. With her head dropped and arms at her sides. Ridiculous!

You shouldn't make fun of the child.

I'm not. I am the child.

You?

Yes, I am. Though I'm also the listener. And—this—(holding up her needled arm) as well.

Mira

Research is a mode of existence. How we wander into erasure.

She stops partially into the writing, wondering what reading could pull her out.

A red herring. How many books of promise. Sentinels.

Thought is secondary to taste. There is nothing clever in staying inside a word garden until something recants intent. The fingers crumble or become indelible. What sprouts from our decibel is no longer an ear fit for wrapping.

Where are the places in the book which lag and lack? How to re enter? Will they speak to me? I have been absent so long.

Not knowing what to read, who to become.

Mira & Gray

Pulled? By who or what?

He doesn't wish to say as he looks at her and looks quickly away, as if she could see through him, into his thought. So transparent at that moment. So as almost to have no substance besides that which she possibly saw. But he restrained his thoughts from moving in that direction. The direction, he knew, was endless and led nowhere he might follow in the real tangible corridors and rooms of daily intercourse. And so he stood suspended, *longer than I can tell you,* he thought, compiling an indescribable distance. A length between what one knows in the body, viscerally, like a plummeting stone, clearly as a road or a line has been drawn but which cannot be spoken. And in this abrupt and dramatic manner she spoke to him, or so he thought. What is thought? She spoke to him saying nothing at all. With simply a straightforward gaze.

Still, he had to answer the question. How to be honest without being too revelatory. Clearly it was no fault of hers. He looked into the eyes of his catalyst briefly, and then spoke.

I am in a dark corridor, filled with people, and some-one who I can't clearly see is clasping my hand and pulling me somewhere.

Where?

I don't know.

How does it feel?

He paused again. Imagining Buzz, their unspoken ap-prenticeship, of which he'd told her nothing. It wasn't simple to describe. He said only, like dying—but also . . .

What do you mean?

It's the unknown, but the person who is leading me is someone I trust.

And you are willing to see?

He hadn't thought about this question exactly. Or if he had it hadn't been consciously. He said, It isn't pos-sible to do anything else.

It would be. But that is what you meant by dying, isn't it? Dying is the unwillingness to live. To live is to be in the unknown corridor.

He thought, It is unbearable, this being someone else. Being not you.

But you are, she said, as if she had heard.

This shook him. He said nothing. She took his hands.

It is easy to confuse, she said. But you are able to distinguish the difference. There is only one wish, in which all others reside.

Mira & Gray

I currently live nowhere.

It isn't true Gray. You are here.

Within this, what?

What do you mean?

The Institute is pulsing. It is—

We need an alternate entrance. Where are you?

Try this, she said, and then she turned down a corridor.

She was turning and all he could do was to follow her shoulder. This means of travel, he thought, what is it?

She turned, as if in response. She turned again and he followed. He thought about all of the books he had read with no comprehension at all.

Not true, she thought, turning again to make sure he had not been lost.

How do you do that, he wanted to ask, but speech was kept from him.

Not true, she echoed again.

So I can speak and then I did understand, but not on the level of events. I couldn't have drawn you a map or told you what had happened in a pivotal moment.

Yes, she shot back, But what you did delineate, what did you? Apply that to this. To the Institute. To what you do know now.

And she kept moving, but were they moving? He blinked.

Now open your eyes, she said, We're here.

Here meaning a natural space which had not been disposed of. Where are we, he asked?

There were rocks and open space, a few cushions and a low table set out on a rug with tea. He didn't bother to ask her again.

Please sit, she said, pouring pale liquid into a small ceramic vessel. He watched the steam and said nothing.

You say you couldn't draw it, but you have entered it, she said.

Or it has entered me.

Exactly what has? What is it Buzz has given you, here, embedded in your skin?

If I knew that, entirely—.

You don't know?

No, but—.

But what?

But I'm not entirely unaware either.

He held up his palm again then placed it around the cup and drank. Finally it came to him, only surfaces.

Surfaces?

They have shown me plenty of surfaces. The surfaces of projects, of people, of intentions. But the place beneath the neat agendas—I've had no glimpse.

They couldn't possibly. That is why it has been embedded. So what you know from embedding is what is beneath the surfaces. But how you assess the information, where you take it is what you become.

I don't know what it means.

You aren't entering it completely. Fall into the stream of numbers. Tell me where it takes you. Give me your hand.

He held up his hand and she pressed her palm to the lighted perimeter. She closed her eyes. And after a moment, No, she said, Non-transferable.

Dear Advisor,

There is only one wish

Book Three:

Bea

(Weight of Light)

"Naturally, only those who can think
can travel by thought"
Laura Moriarty

"In a world without sky,
land becomes an abyss.
Is the impossible far?"
Mahmoud Darwish

Bea

The landscape held her, though she did not live in this landscape any longer. Who would ring to remind her oddly. If I do not answer it will be——. If I do answer it will be who I cannot bear to become. I cannot become this name. I can become this prism of blotchy trees. I am allergic to your reactions regarding how the child is to be held. I am allergic to your description of things. Bea thought through these conundrums as she continued through her day of continuous actions. Her arms hold the baby. Her arms lay the baby down to dress him, to undress him. To wipe his dimpled chin. Her legs pulse to calm him as she bounces. The baby breathes rhythmically with his mother. She counts his breaths as they lengthen away from cries and into slumber. She thinks, *I am not separate from him.* She tries to imagine him one day running. This is impossible. Toddlers are incomprehensible giants. Speaking children are alien entirely. She has become her child temporarily, but the motion is complete and intact, just as her careful stacking away of all of those things which for now he may not touch, scissors and knives, heavy things, precarious lamps, dangling cords. The space is orchestrated, arranged for the crawling consciousness, the oral minded. Repetition is all. He crawls toward the cold dirty fireplace. She lifts him away. How many times may she do this?

She thinks, I am allergic to the world which does not understand me now. And all of those adults who have forgotten that they were once children and this invisible work which will translate the future. She thinks, translate the future, and all of the infants and how will they arrange the future? The future is in our care, if we will deliberately bear it.

My child is (or my children are) every age they have been up until this present. Do not expect me to forget his, or your, or anyone's infancy. Or future.

Let us discuss codes for disciplinarian constraints, for walking. Nanoprobes inserted into the skin of the child which inform the office as a result of the child leaving the premises. A school is religiously regarding your skin color. A school is assuming it is okay to yell at your child in public if you are culture A. Based upon behavior your child is given a color.

Bombarded by: pull-out guide to day camps, on the clock or by demand, choosing a college, massive play, team parties, group trips, fund raisers, scouting events, carpentry for kids, does your child have the importance of groups? Learning disabilities, convertible cribs, wouldn't you like a home of your own? Weaning your toddler from problems ahead, affordable therapy, gear drive drop off locations, hire the best, does your boy like to sing?, cathedral school for boys, sign up now for appleseed day, the salamander shuffle, open water, green stuff, information fair.

Interlude:

PC: Salamander shuffle, yes.

HJ: I don't do carpentry.

She cannot see what is evolving, even if it isn't.

You can understand it one way, but another too which is the way of later when you are someone.

This is about the future which is also now.

Then why shall we rush with putting on your socks. There must be a character who is a mother and for whom being a mother is not a small anecdotal detail, thought the mother, who did have a name she could not quite remember at that moment.

The mother had a name and the name had a color, and a sound. But for now, the softness of her child's feet had succumbed. She had succumbed to them. Start taking notes she told herself, taking notes now, pulling the sock onto his foot, while he laughed and wiggled away.

But why shall I, she wondered. What can one accomplish in this way? Don't be so transparent then, or shall I?

Something is evolving, even if it isn't. And, I might miss it. Your own birth for instance, says the child. You were an infant, and now look at you. The child denies this. The child has a voice and he avidly denies ever having been an infant. In the same way, the mother thinks, that adults deny education should be allocated sufficient funds so that schools are not a catastrophe. But it is not in the same way. The child does so innocently.

If all time is happening now, your foot in the sock, legs out the door, down the red steps, into the car and off to school clutching lunchboxes, one clean blanket for rest time, homework, permission slip, five dollar bill. Phone, sunglasses, water. Clutching this.

What can one accomplish in this way? Don't be so momentary, or shall we?

Bea

To work—I must find my virtual brushes, my diatonic paints, my screens and my protective eyewear, needing to be replaced, cracked about the edges where my little one stepped upon them, pulled from my bag and my shoulder and fallen to the floor.

Code, enter.

She looks up to the retinal screener, steps down upon the moving lift which will carry her to her station, high above the ground facing, today, she notes as she arranges her computer palate and other instruments upon her person, a particularly remote corner of the quadrant. She is lifted up and almost has what she thinks of as a memory. First she feels the warmth of the sun. And then she remembers it clearly. Looking up into the sun. And though this couldn't possibly be true, the memory persists.

She insists, contrary to common belief, that such a memory must be protected. And that it could not be constructed entirely from her imaginings. She believes in a human recognition, an internal map, of the sort once discovered in the eye of an ant, or in the navigational instincts of birds. Human beings know sun. If she feels its warmth she can conjure the image. Even though she is told how much safer the atmosphere is now. Even then, she would rather her children grew up with a memory like this one, which she believes, she must have inherited.

The notion of inherited memory is controversial still, and yet despite the lack of evidence available to support the theory, Bea believes it with certainty. Of course the promoters of the Future View would want to denigrate any remains, and remorse, any regret which had been painstakingly manufactured and deliberately embedded in the next generation in order to inspire a vast undraping, an undoing of the protective systems now in place. Of course there are those who want to save dying languages, dying landscapes. Of course we have the potential to change what we have changed again. And to see differently, if we choose.

But all of this was very briefly thought by Bea, who had reached her station where the work was begun which silenced her thoughts. The mere repetitive nature of her task, the watchfulness required didn't leave much else of her mind to consider. She had initially hoped that it might. All sense of toil had been evidently scrubbed from the job description by the Department of Veneer Illustration. There was the promise of serenity even. This prevarication she occasionally wondered about as she stood on a brief scaffolding where she was accountable for rendering her ripple of what once would have been called "sky." There was an elaborate screen above her head which demanded various movements and changes in the scene as the hours progressed. This too, worked against her instincts. The rhythm of a day, so it was argued by various promoters, would be so much more interesting if the scene were to change more often. Persons are not interested in such flatness, in slow changing weather patterns. And so Bea changed her palette again and again. She was to stand for a fifteen-hour shift. This was possible with nutrition tablets and mineral vials and the new form of sleep prescribed by most physicians termed "pharmaceutical rest." *In which we are rested sooner*, chimed the promotional song. *Wouldn't you like to be rested sooner? The human body is capable of so much.*

But there were other things which interested Bea more, other things the body was capable of, and not merely the body. What of the rest of us, she wondered, for a brief instant standing—a thin rail upon her scaffold, wondering over her children's education between glimpses at the veneer's attire schedule. Her palette was arranged for the hour and moved directly through her fingertips and various paddles and brushes. Her arms were in motion nearly all day. When she glimpsed the other workers on their stations above and below she could imagine they were speaking a language with their arms. She could almost feel the exhaustion of all of them utterly. And this facade goes on, she thought. And why must it? But the next moment she was lost in it. The color, the movement. She had a secret which sustained her through these efforts. But then the thought was lost again and replaced with exertion and bewilderment at the question of whether anyone were truly watching.

She misses the notion of birds—birds would have been watching—most have been obliterated, could not tolerate the false sky which filters the dangerous rays and pollutants. It was a small price to pay, say the experts, to save us from such hazards. And what is lost, they ask, considering real light does penetrate the curtain of the Future View.

She presses her keypad closed. She lowers her arms and looks smiling at the last bit of violet upon her screen. Then she steps upon a lever and begins to descend from her shift. Her elbows tingling. She looks down at the retinal screener. She steps out and is given her copy of the Department Bulletin, which she scans that evening dutifully, after the children have gone to sleep. Today there is a piece upon the sweat shops of the twentieth and twenty-first centuries.

She goes now slowly to the news, to wash her hands again and again, to wash off the custom of the day, in which she stands within the unreal tent, blinking in the false light which stings the eyes—painting waves of wind, cunning, adjusting the sound, so each moment is distinct. The veneer is thin between herself and the outside. The true outside for which she can only wave at the blackness. She cannot remember how things were once different but there is in that vast darkness a possibility of revival. She wants to step underneath, to touch. There are warnings that this is dangerous, that the land is toxic, that she is much safer on the fabricated ground, but again and again, she thinks of going beneath.

Then she goes home and considers herself lucky to have her children, to have a rented room, to be away from the falseness. To fall into the natural darkness. And as she reads, she considers herself lucky because she is not like those persons in the past who worked in airless factories, with dangerous machines, she is not going blind from small stitching. She considers herself safe, as she reads about:

Workers being fired for attempting to unionize.

Serious work injuries as daily occurrences. Broken fingers, lacerated hands, broken legs, deaths.

Workers locked in the factory compound 10 to 13 hours a day.

Living in one-room huts, many without windows, without running water or electricity.

Selling their blood plasma to survive.

Facing mandatory pregnancy tests.

She reads about the basic costs of survival for a family of four, and its means: rent, electricity, water, propane gas, food, babysitter. The total weekly income earned falls short of these basic expenses.

She reads and is grateful to have departed from those barbaric centuries.

The Future View has ended all of this, she thinks. What else has it ended? What newly is concealed, in all of the blankness of safety, nutritional tablets, lack of dirt, of perspiration, of recognition? Why are minerals to be found only in colored vials?

One day she sees something which startles her. An invisible child is standing outside the entrance to her workplace holding her safety goggles in the air and reciting:

"*Seal my eyes. Seal my eyes from sight of the view once apparent, no longer contagious contaminants. Seal my eyes. Says the potion, we are taunted to read before entering our workplace. Put on your protective eyewear. What must we not see?*"

Bea thinks, So I am told, the precaution of goggles is merely that until materials can be further assessed. There are preventative paints which do not deteriorate with time. I must look at them day after day.

And when I awake, unseal my eyes. When I step out from the tent and the curtain. I see the eyes of my child. I awaken, and even before I enter the curtain I reach instinctively for my goggles.

When Bea questions her, the child puts on her goggles and turns to face her.

"Go," says the invisible child, "and have your eyes

examined."

She is only permitted to work here because she is invisible, Bea thinks, certain that she is a child. So that is the new way in which children are used. And how did they become invisible?

Slowly, selectively forgetting the presence of what is necessary for a child to be seen.

Bea imagines, you could draw them this way. With a bow in the hair. With a shoelace and a shoe below. And nothing else between.

You don't need to clothe them. They don't need guardians either, since no one wishes to bother with a race of invisible persons. It is so much less rewarding she is told, to raise an invisible child. And will they ever be seen again?

Bea brought the invisible child home, to play with her visible children. She brought her home and by the end of the evening the lower part of her legs had become visible. And then the child wrote out some information upon a little card. And she asked Bea to see a healer of eyes who uses distinct and indistinct therapies to test what they had been told was an imagined affliction. An imagined affliction experienced only by workers upon the Future View. In a time when workers are safe, transparently, according to the world media.

Bea

It would have destroyed her to be separated from a small child running through some newly laid cement in front of the school. Because of his curls and his furtive eyes and because time is passing, because of the cost of fixing the cement, and because she shouldn't compare herself to another, to a mother in a book, or standing beside her. Yet to know this is to know her: it would have destroyed her to be separated from her children. Yet she is separated and lives.

Her story is this: primal, accompanied by difficult sleeping or eating. A full-time or nearly half-time or how much away time she was constantly negotiating in her mind. And the guilt of others' satisfaction is also what will be regretted once you have the job and the child is grown, she thought. So she was able to suffer in the future as well as in the present. Then there was the present pain: to imagine them lacking. Therefore she found no plausibility or comfort in the fantasy of never being parted.

In infancy, she argued, we were, are, the same person. The joy in that being with one's child is existence. What is true? Simply to look into their eyes. She didn't know she was chosen for this thought experiment, she only knew that she had proven, beyond any doubt that she remained separate only as an illusion.

Not owning her thoughts also destroyed her. Something fierce which she did not wish to recognize in herself emerged during the long shifts. She had yet to name it. Yet she separated her thoughts, her options, and her whereabouts. She noted something else had separated. Fingers fell apart, eyes attempted to look in different directions, bodies were difficult to locate. Did the torn aperture exist inside, or merely around them?

Bea

Today scent of cardamom cures all and the list end-less, how to grasp and still to remain within time. Not to be merely the person crossing off what must be done.

Work is an amalgam of thinking. If I am prevented from thought a scent of cardamom draws me back. The breath of a boy, his hand in mine, we cross the street. Whose birth is approaching. We know this and therefore abbreviate nothing. Between cooking and exhaling, a practice built upon where we are to live in the future.

The moment of picking them up is such a bright moment. And so confusing. Never having accomplished what I'd thought.

Thought is a medium difficult to describe. Still, we think in it. What difference does it make how many skies I may design? She looks up, and sees the wisp of a moving patch of clouds she has created.

Do you know where we're going, she anticipates asking the driver? The driver meaning, the one steering her own consciousness, as she stands waiting in front of the blue door, beside the other mothers, in her slightly worn shoes.

Reading you is intersecting. You—meaning the absent. The world is rash and blight. I am not what you call ravished. Furthermore, the world is this work and something is gripping. Where my children become and gather themselves. So listen.

This evolves in its own primacy.

It is difficult to remember that correspondence is and isn't my work. Research is a mode of existence. How we wander into erasure.

Partially into the thought she stops. How many books of promise. Therefore who we have become. Sentinels.

Thought is secondary to immersion, taste. There is nothing clever in staying inside a word garden until something recants intent. The fingers crumble or become edible. What sprouts from your decibel is no longer an ear fit for wrapping.

Where are the places which lag and lack? How to re enter s-k-y? Will it speak to me? I have been absent so long.

Not knowing what to draw, who to become.

Interlude:

M: You are never absent from s-k-y.

Bea

Bea attending to unheard bills and buttering kitchens. Sending out this or that recycled notion in a returning call. Scattering ashes of disbelief that they have grown so. As she hears the length and breadth of their play. At the same time she is collecting something, arranging something else. Her hands move with or without the matter they oblige. The ongoing nature of these orchestrations never fails to surprise her. She is learning to allow weariness to enter. She stops for a moment, to listen at the door. They are sitting attentively listening to the invisible child, who is only visible at the moment on account of the bow in her hair which bobs almost audibly as she animates her tale. Bea crawls between the many legs to sit entwined in their warmth. Their innocence bathing her. Breath and arms without thought encircle her. A head is upon her chest. The tale has not at all lulled.

The invisible child continues:

———

Though they both have reason to resist, they do not. And she thinks she has found what she is longing to learn, briefly, she has a glimpse of it. And he thinks, *No matter the consequences, so long as we may be horizontal.*

————————————————

Bea untangles herself from her children who leap up into play. She takes the hand of the invisible child and leads her out of the room.

This is not a story for children.

The bow nods and drops several feet to the ground. Bea sits beside her.

Where did you find it?

The bow nods from side to side. And then she opens her mouth to speak. She closes her mouth again. Bea can hear the exhalation. Then the bow rises and bounces across the room to her knapsack. She bounces back clutching a book.

The Malady of Love

Memoirs of Starla, a Space Ranger

Chapter

The problem with employers is that if she were to learn anything she would always then fall in love with her employer. This was a nuisance to her. At first, she believed it was the fault of the employer, but when the happening repeated itself with two other employers she began to notice that she was not capable of not loving her employer. One described it to her like this, "Ah my flower." But that was no description at all, as far as she was concerned, of what had happened to her. What was it that she could not help? This seemed a question worth serious attention, and yet no one, especially not her employers, could tell her anything about it.

Chapter

He, oblivious, was in another land.

Chapter

To say I simply wish to be in your presence could be misinterpreted.

Chapter

I could have so easily trespassed. No, I did not. And what does it mean to have someone continue to cross your path? Again and again. Non-incident.

Chapter

Can I tell you a secret?

He gazes at her, says nothing, but his gaze allows her to go on.

Chapter

He holds the book in front of them.

They collapse and the book falls to the ground.

Chapter

I want something you can't give me. This isn't meta-phorical.

Chapter

It is all we think about or talk about. My imaginary conversations are many. I don't know where to begin. I believe there is a whole world of history between us.

How is this a malady?

Chapter

You'd think all of this would make someone happy. But it didn't. Something always crashes, she says.

Chapter

She stops to think. Is a mere process of deduction enough? Is her plan sound, to love every person she ever meets, in rapid succession, ruling out inappro-priate choices, until finally—?

And from where does it come, this voracious capacity to love?

Chapter

It looks different in fantasy than pressed up against the glass of a chance meeting.

Chapter

They met on the street.

Chapter

It is easier on paper.

Chapter

They met on a blind date in which she, thinking herself with an optometrist, brought her entire collection of used eyeglass frames. Pulling them one after another from a bag and placing them on her face, as if to ask.

She did not know that the optometrist had not yet

arrived. So who was this man sitting across from her, obviously amused?

Did it matter?

Chapter

When the optometrist arrives, he isn't happy.

Chapter

Who will instruct me?

Chapter

The reason you cannot see it is that you have covered it.

Chapter

I need to know something. What is your real name? And what is mine?

Chapter

The telephone line is engaged again and again she cannot get through and so she goes out and meets someone else.

Chapter

What I want I cannot name. It can be easily mistaken for you.

Bea

Bea cannot stop reading the book.

This is curious, Bea says. She has learned to think that the invisible child is not a child. That the sky is not the sky. That a house is not a house. I cannot understand it, she says. How is she able to love each character she comes across?

Only her knees are visible now. She crosses them, and laughs. She loves nobody completely. Isn't it the same as loving everybody?

Bea wonders what has happened to this child, that she could see such a thing. I don't see it, she says.

You are the other face of love. The invisible child looks up.

Bea looks in astonishment for the first time at the face of the child, which is revealed for an instant. And in her eyes she sees the recognition she has sought for some time from this enigmatic little being. As quickly as the vision appears it also vanishes.

Bea's Notebook

1

Invisible feeds the visible.

My children begin the day. Witch picture fell off of the wall. The bony-fence cereal. He sees a squirrel-bat on the way to school.

This non-material light, as I imagine it is filtering, though the shades are closed, and falling onto the face of a photograph.

2

This is said and unsaid

the known

I could speak of you

but when you arrived
sunlight, medicinal

I call you by such a name

3

Dear Blankness,

Your utterance mistakes me
I am here otherwise blemished by thought
Undone by lack
Timeliness is utterance
If you were to speak through these tracings of words

I say tracing as I am trying to locate the underlines
a scaffolding built upon that unmentionable s-k-y

If I speak I will be scattered as any terse ink
Body transposed

Smudging in a reverie of sand

Have you ever—?

4

Dear—,

Have you ever
lain awake by fingerlight
of the one no longer
beside you?

5

Retire, when to revere, pay reverence to expiring tickets and registrations, the endless formatting of motherhood, return this, staple that, the folders and the string to wind about plastic wheels. Costume, *check*, permission slip, *check*, mineral vials, *check*. You still forgot the pledge money, the sharing day, *check*, mental angst, *check*, those who consider you to be daycare for their children, *check*, please pick him up by five o'clock, *check*. Five o'clock. No one arrives, *check*. Five-thirty, phone call, *check*. We are sitting down to dinner with how many additionals? The invisible child, *check*. You can hardly blame them, *check*.

Bedtime, bath, teeth. Paid rent, *check*. What is forgotten twice?

Returned call, voting research, the desk, half hidden in all means of significant communications mixed with research, *check*.

Who have you become? By the middle of the day. *Check*. This isn't a memory, it is today. But then again, as I lay here in the imagined sunlight, so forbidden, so evidently normal—that bodies recline.

6

If you admit to me in all good humor the evident
trouble you cause, especially since your absence, I
will smile, and take you to bed.

Let your hair grow
Fall down to your knees
Remember scent

We once inhabited *now* for many hours
Weeks in which we planned for this unconsigned

Continually arriving future

Awakening together by habit and necessity
How long before they will wake us?

Remedies for unanswerable questions
why you have been taken
Now that such inquiry permeates
My every thought

And my meter has turned to ask
Everything

A Memory of Sunlight

Bea, stands upon her station

Hands perplexed for a pause

She is watching something, tracking a dark filament
of—

Therefore, she speaks to her fingers

o

Dark filament of crowd. Of counter-culture. The word
is gone. Whatever it is. I am certain it has been stolen.
This is different than never having had whatever it
was. A thought. A place name carved into reverbera-
tory categories. I have read the word c-l-o-u-d. I have
painted such contusions on what was once s-k-y. Am
I forbidden to know these words as more than his-
tory? Here I may tell you, filament of *cloud*. *Sky*. I am
forbidden to remember, but instructed to draw. To
reconstruct based upon the drawings and programs
before me.

But once my instructions have been completed for whichever shift I am supposed I will take off those spectacles guarding something I dare not wish to know. I take off my industrious glaring personage which affords me this place of rest.

Who will soon become the future? Once I have taken off all of these accoutrements I sometimes forget what is beneath. What was my intention in writing into such emptiness? In speaking to you in all fullness of raiment which lies beneath a garb. Once I have forsaken where I have been, where I am becomes suspect.

I am writing to you in the hope that I am writing to someone.

What is this remembrance?

If I could fall into this, reverence, for what was—.

What is it I ask myself, my hands, what has crossed, what I am attempting to paint and therefore murder? No I am told by another, it is rendering. I am standing in an antiquated kitchen. There are no longer kitchens. But the memory persists. Alchemy is of another kind.

Whose hands and a memory of sunlight. I tried to

explain it to my children, sitting on a ledge, legs bobbing back and forth.

It would be falling onto your knees, I said.
How can something of no substance fall, they asked.
And how would you know?
It would be heat, pleasant. Not simply the surface. I have seen plants turn their faces to it. I say, in time-lapse film.

It fell and it fell
I cannot see it
Can you taste it?

This didn't work, my explanations

o

She is interspersing her hands with her writings, just as if she could replace a notion which is irreplaceable but once so common so as to be invisible. Natural light, as if we were to hold a clear pane of glass in front of us, and looking through fail to see it.

It had not existed in her lifetime. Who will plunder the unrecoverable instance in order to become this thing? The light penetrates but is mediated by something which has not been revealed.

Bea's Notebook

Dear Transparency of Future Light,

1. There is light in the future. I have seen this and recant.

2. There is a secret tunneling, which must be told to someone.

3. Since the "you" of my imaginings is absent I know you must be listening. The door is open and sleep is near to me.

4. If I tell this by any other means I may be silenced.

5. I have a memory which is not believed.

6. Writing into this is speaking. Will you be able to read through white space?

7. While my children sleep I become another animal akin to awakening, though I am sleep incarnated.

8. Such sleep is not to be believed. It is pumped into me, as if I were something to be consumed.

9. My notes concern the Future View. What I paint is not an antiquated redundancy. It is a memory.

10. When the artificial light moves I remember something which is not artificial.

11. These patterns must be made of something. Why have we been dressed and addressed so carelessly? I must begin somewhere.

12. What is your name?

13. This is how memory behaves. Like a name you have always known. An address, a face. Suddenly vanished. Like light.

Book Four:

i

The Hidden Book
of the Institute

Prelude:

Buzz:

Decode the genetic text

Gray:

The movement of persons is the hidden text

Mira:

Live by the letters, invocational, directional

Bea:

Repaint the text of sky

HJ:

Corridors of text are my favored manner of travel

CL:

You exist within the text as a magnetic precursor

Gray

Gray is angling. He holds up his hand and sees a series of perforations, marking a tiny square in his palm. As he holds it closer he notices the perforations are lit.

With his other hand he claps the lit palm down upon his knee. Am I ill, he wonders. Though he does not really consider the possibility. Staggering to sit. Holding up his hand again, unmistakable red points aglow describing a square in his palm.

He needs to lie down. Various thoughts rush through his head as quickly as he dismisses them: environment sickness, contaminated mineral vials, respiration toxins. Now he begins to calm. Nothing ails him exactly. Hallucinations?

But then he remembers the little black square. Embedded in skin.

He is the modern safe, code, computer.

Why didn't they warn me, he wonders, now holding up his hand more quizzically. And what if I were not alone when this was to happen?

This had been on the first day he had arrived. Besmirched and knowing nothing. Thinking now how little he knew, but that was a different nothing altogether.

There are questions which cannot be answered and yet we ask them.

He thinks of Buzz, whose explanation had been lost upon him the same day. *It has its own intelligence. The process has already begun involuntarily.*

Gray breathed and tried to fathom the glowing screen of his palm.

Just another tunnel, he thought. Another passage perhaps this time revealed?

He holds up his hand

Beginning, transmission. . .

Prelude:

Merchant of the phosphorescent wars

Defenders who teacheth me so gently

With such fair allurement

Licking virologists wounds

Fasting, to partake not of genetically modified fields

Flagellation in the form of chemical salves and emollients

Pilgrimages to radioactive laboratories, preserved below ground

Rather than consume

Impress preparedness upon thy hands

Take for test thy nasal swabs

Open not thy mail

Desist the central transports

Shun public squares to dodge pathogens

Draw not from the cryptosporidium well

Practice syndromic surveillance

Report clinical dis-ease observations,

Sold out Imodium

Blood donors assist the science of persuasion

Encrypted Page

Is the Institute good or evil?
Is the Institute lyric?

Institute you
Who has written it?

Stand here and you are very becoming
in this Institutional light

Beyond fluorescent
you are incandescent, transcending categories
bleeding them

No fleece see I upon your garbled sentences
I set up or establish
to get under way
for carrying on a particular work
of scientific character

Shall I be more precise?
I want to dwell in the palace with you

Carbons and chemicals aside
Something instituted or established
as an authoritative legal principle

Come prepared
I have ripped from my innards this song
Though an Institute cannot sing

The Institute Defined

The insane plot rung through the sober courtroom:

1. An establishment devoted to the promotion of a particular object, especially one of a public character

or: Take thousands of powder samples, bars of white, the last two ribs with pointed extremities

2. The building devoted to such work

or: Repeat the name Prudence or Constance, obiter dictum

3. A place of confinement, as a mental hospital

or: Take photographs of the missing, set to memory

4. Any established law, custom, etc

or: Draw the new surrounding map penciling persons in secure locations

5. Any familiar practice or object

or: "Being, thing and something are the first things impressed" upon the fossil skeleton.

Between instinct and instruction you fail

Too many pages within you

You are sunning yourself between them

You paginate encyclopedic allurements

You page irreverent aides

To stand over your shoulder and chide

Now you are unafraid to cut and to blister

Take telephone intercepts, hyaline cartilage

Begin work with completely unrestricted access

Take eyewitness accounts

The predicate term "trigger"

Take military records, crusts of bread, mass graves

Forensic studies, linguistic flowers of mammals

If you delay, obstruct or lie

These terms infuse the altered cells

Back into the subject's bodies.

(aside)

This is so satisfactual

That you are blindly brutally in love with
catastrophic numbers

Interrogatory Interlude:

(Bea and her children)

Why does our water come only in mineral vials, the children ask.

Before there were colored vials——. She is imagining what she thought she once knew.

What was it mommy? I think the vials are pretty

But before there were vials there were. . .

Total renewable freshwater supply
Freshwater withdrawal
Access to safe drinking water
Access to water supply and sanitation by region
Irradiated areas
Number of dams
Waterborne disease outbreaks
Hydroelectric capacity production
Desalination capacity

Estimates of global morbidity and mortality caused by water related disease before the advent of mineral vials:

(episodes per year of persons infected)

Intestinal Helminths	1,500,000,000
Schistosomiasis	200,000,000
Dracunculiasis	150,000
Trachoma	150,000,000
Malaria	400,000,000
Dengue Fever	1,750,000
Poliomyelitis	114,000
Trypanosomiasis	275,000
Bancroftian Filariasis	72,800,000
Onchocerciasis	17,700,000 persons infected; 270,000 persons blinded

These records are not secret but are classified documents in the sense that you never have nor will you ever remember having read them

Dear initiate, I do not ask your forgiveness I am a record

The author has been forgotten

Only the words remember themselves

Again and again you return to the page and then become forgetful

I, the record, am innocent

It will be clear to even the most caustic reader that these deflections are imprecise and that single eventualities can fall into more than one category depending on peregrination and defensiveness. For example, intentional mimetic attacks on mineral-vial supply systems can fall into both the tardy and the tooth and nail categories, depending on one's point of vigil. Disputes over control of mineral-vial resources may reflect either political potable disputes or disagreements over approaches to ecocide development, or both. We believe this is inevitable and even descendent descriptive—international security of mineral-vial supplies is not a clean, precise field of styptic and analogy.

Your thoughts are changing, your assumptions about

daughter cells

Institute Verified Transcription

thousands of powder samples, bars of white

You haven't touched, you haven't inhaled, but you have seen the account again and again and your mirror cells begin to respond. The powder samples are pressed into bars of white suppression. You have not held them but they are accountable for your forgetfulness.

the last two ribs with pointed extremities

These being the ribs of an instrument carved from mirror forgetfulness having inhaled the episode.

mental hospital

You don't remember the mental hospital. You don't remember the musical intimation. You don't remember the powder sample.

missing persons in secure locations

The maps have been hidden. This is for your protection. The identification of these persons has been encrypted.

telephone intercepts

Intercepts were made without proper verification thus obliterated. Everything was overheard.

hyaline cartilage, eye witness, military records, mass graves

Records of the war of resistance, civil war, protestors against the Future View. You don't remember this. You don't remember powder samples, intimations, mental hospitals, the deceased.

Authorship is authority, culpability. This is commonly and erroneously believed. The record is made by no one.

How is the Institute implicated in the mineral vial supply—

You will not remember that the Institute supported the war, the draperies we call s-k-y. The workers in the Institute are not aware of this, have no memory of war, no memory of powder samples, no memory before the Future View.

Mirror Cell Research Abstract
by
Space Ranger
Buzz Lightyear

What is a mirror cell?

Mirror cells mirror. Enter the diagram please. If I reach for a mineral vial I see you doing the same thing in attenuated memory. Your brain cells fire as if you had done it too.

How are mirror cells used in Institute research?

Mirror cells represent the future of sustainable universe systems. For example, preventing scarcity and maintaining purity of mineral vial resources through mirror cells is one line of Institute research.

Our studies have shown that repeated observation of subject A taking sustenance will cause the mirror cells to fire in subject B as if subject B has also taken sustenance. For a short time this cognitive process can feed the body. All Institute staff are being trained in this practice of Mirror cell sustenance as a preventative measure.

Goals: to provide the general public with Mirror Cell survival training.

Note: several early files are encrypted beyond decodability. Original transcriptions have been deleted. Several years of data missing.

Medical Applications:
mental states, aggression retraining, organ functioning (organ to organ speech), nutritive visual processing.

Virtual Applications:
Healing across distances.

Financial Applications:
Increase in shift length, productivity. Lessen need for sleep, meals.

Note:
Empathy is a key component in the functioning of mirror cells.

Research Data

Premise A

On a cold receptacle planetary station in the gamma quadrant a Virtual Companion sat in a special terminal waiting for Researchers to return. Everytime the Companion grabbed an object cells would fire in that region of its brain, registering in a display as a spike on a graph on a nearby screen.

A researcher walked in carrying a memory card containing new information files. The Virtual Companion stared at him. When the researcher opened and began to read the files the monitor showed that the companion's mirror neurons had fired even though the Virtual Companion had only observed the researcher accessing the files, without accessing them himself.

Space Ranger S. earlier noticed the same phenomenon with music and film files, with desirable mineral vials and other objects.

Premise B

The Virtual Companion brain contains a special class of cells called mirror neurons that fire when the Companion sees or hears an action and carries out the same action on its own.

Premise C

Humans have mirror neurons that are more intelligent, supple and more highly evolved than any of those found in Virtual Companions or other life forms.

The human brain contains multiple mirror neuron systems which can decode not just the movements of others but their intentions as well as emotions which impel the actions.

"We are exquisitely social beings," Lightyear said. "Mirror neurons allow us to grasp the minds of others not through conceptual reasoning but through direct simulation. By feeling, not thinking."

Insula Circuits
&
Von Economo Neurons
or
VENS

Her insula is damaged, Buzz suggested.

Excuse me? Gray felt the color rising again. No end to this sea of what wasn't known. Where have I been, he asked himself? How must I immerse myself?

Buzz looked at him oddly. Her VENS are damaged beyond repair.

Meaning?

Buzz studied him quizzically. Follow me, he said. And they proceeded down another corridor. One behind the stylized door which looked like—what did it look like? The body of an instrument, he thought, An instrument wearing a corset. A fortress garment. A forest girded. But just then the whole contraption descended and they stepped through a portal into an entirely blue room.

Blue, said Buzz. Here we are looking at color and sound. How insula damaged subjects respond.

Gray thought about the Future View, the dense blue palettes of paints which do not deteriorate. How many of these VENS damaged subjects have worked on the Future View, he asked?

Buzz glared at him but did not answer immediately. How many unheard of corridors, he thought.

And then, reluctantly, he answered, All of them.

How many unheard of, undocumented corridors of hidden research, thought Gray. Then he felt the blue of the walls assault him.

Oh, sorry, said Buzz, noting Gray's tremor, I forgot you haven't been de-sensitized. He handed Gray a pair of goggles.

This did something to the color. It descended an octave, yet somehow it was more contagious, toned down but more suffused. He thought, I am breathing it now, instead of seeing it, while he tried to keep pace down the blue hallway.

The color is twice as nuanced here, said Buzz.

Gray looked through the glass and saw a young woman sitting in front of a field of blue projected upon a screen in front of her. She was sitting so still and staring intently, no expression.

Severely VENS damaged, Buzz bent over and whispered, and then he walked further along. Past several purpled latticeways and dark flowing curtains. Eventually he turned and lifted one of the coverings. One way glass, he said.

Gray saw a man encased in a booth wearing headphones, curled over in what looked like wrenching pain. What's the matter with him, Gray asked.

Buzz looked back down the corridor at Gray, his eyes looking menaced but also sorry. Nothing, he said.

Gray

This would all be explained to me later (so I was told). In this transcription of my notes on the Institute I can only describe *later* as a type of plaster—taking form, becoming less malleable, constrictive. What gives support to a notion may also keep it immobile. *Certain is nothing*, is the motto of the manual. I read to keep pace with my questions.

The insula is located on two sites in the brain, the insula, your social glue, what evokes music with emotion, or you, with desire. Not merely the act of drinking but the design of the lip as it does so. To stand holding a bottle in a sitting room and to maintain a particular anticipatory breathing pattern before doing so, before gazing at or touching your desired _____. Before anything, the Insula, buried deep in the brain, once thought not to exist, is being retaught, or so it is the hope of the Institute now to be able to retrain Insula sensitivity for those who have lost their capacity for empathy.

My question is, how were they damaged? The Insula damaged patients? How did it occur?

But more intently it comes to me audibly, like a blue wall tipping to sea, buried, trammeled, did they wish to keep it from me? They are using the research to change how it works. To manipulate, so that we won't suspect the Future View. Instead we will emote as we once did for s-k-y. Just a visual plane, occurring in history. You don't remember, chime the invisible probes.

But my other non-probed voice interrupts. Notion of inherited memory? Question of human subjects in research? By choice or coercion? And are they protected? Compensated? Who is responsible?

What of the notion of implanted memory, reverted, encrypted, corrupted, stolen proclivity to remember, to advance thinking, to draw a pronounced independent conclusive emotive response to a situation?

Implanted and obliterated memory, are they being used then to motivate, infiltrate? Why was there no resistance to the draping of the sky? Why was there no resistance to the control of mineral vial supplies by the Institute?

Is resistance something then which requires empathy? Empathy requires unmutilated Insual function.

The probed subjects respond, This is in the new history.

Whose history, I ask?

Book Four

ii

"As For the Future"

Mira & Gray

Your research is in a book?
Not a book
On the body?
In a manner of speaking
Speaking how?
I was mistaken.
Meaning?
About the mineral vials

These, she reaches into her pocket?

And also the Future View

Ghastly thing—I can't get used to it

What do you mean—used to it?

Where I come from—

Where do you come from?

She smiles, thinking *I cannot recount my previous lives.* She says, you wouldn't believe me. But there was none of this. These pretty vials. Severely unsatisfying.

Mira, what are you saying?

Severely. She walks out saying not another word

But Mira, what was it then, in place of these things, this sustenance?

She ignores the question and says, vile humans de-stroying unspeakable, losing s-k-y, o-c-e-a-n

Those words have no meaning. We've never glimpsed them.

Have you ever seen—? She stops, says nothing, drops the vials one by one, exits the Institute

He follows.

She turns to walk away

Let me come with you

She turns back, begins to speak—Your task—

He looks at her, uncertain, asks, how will I know?

You will collide. It will be unmistakable.

Interlude:

M: Your task is *definitely* not what you suppose it to be.

CL: If you would only stop supposing anything then we might begin.

HJ: I do not wish to visit this ridiculous future.

PC: You are a coward!

Mira's Lament

Everyone has a memory of sunlight. And since it has been lost, inexplicably, I must recount here.

There is a way of writing this which does not suppose anything is written. I have to sing it. But from where I come singing thus not to lament but to praise. How am I to praise the absence of light? And the absence of the memory of light?

Dear Advisor, upon what decibel of acreage must I write? Upon which downy hillock must I recline to feel the lack of light falling upon my decimated skin?

No mineral vials suppose water, luxuriant elixir of which we are principally constructed.

But this too has been forgotten.

Water-diamond paradox, do you walk with less oxygen now?

The Future View is upon us.

The vial (vile) place must recant.

I even would desire the life I revoked
where water and light, once abundant.

In the past—where we must invent the future.

Mira to Bea

Once upon a scaffolding she stands

Holding her non-illuminated arms out

To flutter in front of her

Once within a mineral vial she quaffed

She feeds the memory of water and light

Catalyst for the memory of one

One is a world

One must be enough

Starla

This new dwelling by the Future View. I've come to the end of something beginning. Is it movement and I accumulating clouds to hear about a nuisance? Zurg kept saying it would happen. He said, Don't joke, as if our assumptions were made true by him saying my name once loudly, by taking our places as we did so many times, as if by osmosis. As if another person could edit this concept of distance—instead Zurg is transferred. I am transferred. Finally away from chaos of his design. And who was Gray? Another pawn, another frame, another falling, failing.

This isn't nearly all of it either. Still not falling to sleep would be fine but for waking. Remembering how long it took me to avoid and now to have arrived there is no not seeing oneself is there? Do I need new mental attire, orange with a little gold vyed thread, such as I glimpsed upon so and so? But what does one need this for? To avoid the inner snows. Parched ice. Thaw. Reminders. The saw. Back and forth. Ice. But to recall my former domicile. I push. I mend. I am not being asked easily. Some bend.

Starla was expecting Buzz for nourishment. She busied herself with all of her things. There was arranging the sound in hypnotic drone from various rooms.

There was slightly veiling the Future View. There were the projections of color along the walls. But none of these things fit into her new dwelling which was less sleek than her previous cell and atmospheric only in a distinctly unplush manner. A manner not natural to Starla, but which she had imagined would suit her very well. There was the table set with tablets in mesh pouches, vials of minerals infused with scent. There was the incoherent table bloom, and yet though she saw these things she tried not to see them with the firm intention of appearing at ease.

Should she turn up the volume upon the path determinator, to hear if he were coming? No, how dreadful to hear nothing. Or to hear someone passing on their way elsewhere. Or even, walking away, becoming almost inaudible. Then, she caught the sound of her thinking and paused. I mustn't mention any of this to Buzz, she thought, somewhat appalled at the turn her thought had taken. As if they, her thoughts, had, in the absence of other company, become tangible bodies which escorted her down an interpass she'd had no intention of entering.

The path determinator echoed loudly. Starla was at her entrance in seconds and had applied to her face as she strode boldly what she supposed to be the correct expression for greeting visitors. She began to speak immediately as she opened the door, about the weather and the Future View and the remains of the research season according to the swells.

This annoyed Buzz, who thought, She needs an audience more than usual it appears, catching her complexion put on and the odd array of sound and light he was to enter. But he said aloud, How lovely to see you my dear. And then set right to his blinking attachments and lowered his wings.

They sat down at the table and Starla was so glad to have company that she talked endlessly and spilled almost all of the vials of scented minerals. Then she laughed at the effect upon the table bloom.

Buzz said something kind about the mesh pouches and the quality of the nourishment tablets but about the table bloom he said nothing.

Starla continued on, but after a spell fell silent. At this moment the Future View became exceedingly bright, even in its partially veiled state. The light was red and when it hit the minerals upon the table it turned the surface muddy.

Buzz looked to her desktop and noted that she had been reading a very recent report regarding daughter cells.

Starla replied, Reading some materials make me benevolent, but reading others make me envious. Or even greedy.

Ah, said Buzz, looking down.

This seemed to Starla a retort, as if to say, I am not at all interested in where this is going. But there must be a way to make him understand, she thought. I want my research to determine first, and yet beneath that desire is what I am really wanting to say. I fear something horrid is about to happen. And then I will not have time to accomplish anything. And this brings me back to greed.

The report was not consequential, Starla replied.

Yes, I agree, he responded. And therefore, there is nothing to provoke you to such a degree. He said this somewhat gently and surprised even himself, given the heights of his impatience. If only she could see such self-introspection was the ultimate distraction from her research.

Starla reached for one mineral vial which had not been overturned. She drank it, set it down and somewhat urgently said, Don't you see, this Future View is a veneer of placidity. Some catastrophe is mounting. It has always been mounting. Our dwellings, our research, our sound and color displays seem important and yet they can all be summoned away, in an instant.

Buzz said nothing but raised an eyebrow. Fiddled with his gadgets. Inhaled and exhaled audibly and began to feel his gentleness summoned away.

Starla continued, Some bleakness is approaching and yet one cannot examine it, cannot probe or test, cannot reason or approach. Have you known this? Please tell me you have.

Buzz's wings were stiffening, his chest was blinking and he was beginning to wish he hadn't come. He remarked, There can be sudden conclusions to the universe. But as we cannot predict this, or even approach monitoring the possibility aren't you wasting your time—even to consider?

Starla said nothing and her gaze was somewhat defeated.

Did you read the second amendment to that report, sub theory A attachment, with the diagrams? He asked.

No. I didn't finish. She paused, and then asked, Would you like another vial?

No thank you, he answered. I must be getting back to the Institute shortly.

Yes, I see, she answered. But she made no move to facilitate his departure. She did not rise. Did not look up.

He hadn't seen this side of her. The tangled thought yes, but not the despondency. Maybe, he ventured tentatively, it might be time for your annual maintenance visit? he asked as he stood and pushed in his chair.

Now Starla was angry. And though he saw this, he was relieved to find her despondency had vanished. No, she said. There is something else at work here. You speak about attachments and maintenance, but I am speaking of disaster. Her gaze was pleading with the table bloom. He ignored this.

He said, Have you read the sub attachment B

And she answered, deferring attention, at her wit's display, What do you think of the table bloom? I programmed it myself.

He was now tired, beyond polite behavior. It's vile actually. I'm sorry to say. Just as your morbid preoccupations.

Clearly, she thought, it is time for him to leave. She put on the face for departure.

How mechanical, he thought, she can be. But he was glad to fall into a pattern he could recognize.

Gone was any trace of catastrophe from her face.

Goodbye, my dear, he said.

Thought, An Enmeshed Chapter

(Mira & Gray)

Calcifier, calcified

The oceans absorbed all carbon emissions

Acidification, meaning to say what plummets

Dear Advisor, I fell, and I fell

Your face fell. Our habitable planet

Fell upon the pages

Why is the message incomplete, faltering, failed promise

The first promise is to accept the present

The second promise is to respond appropriately

How can we respond appropriately, he asks, *when we are so busy trying not to see the moment itself?*

Where this ends *dearly—matters*

If you were a calcifier you would find yourself with no shell.

And if you were a reef you would be bleached.

So preoccupied with the defunct s-k-y that we did not consider the o-c-e-a-n.

You speak those forbidden words. Or are they merely forgotten?

The largest living body, covering so much of present-tense reality

What is the shape of this not at all failed promise?

Insistence to hush

That I or you may move

So we set out to paying attention

Turn to ancient texts

Persons were still murdering each other, he points out

Still, to say as if I were moving in a different direction in time

Is time directional, or is that another myth?

You, carbon emitter. You reef bleacher

Numbers can be useful and also territorial

Territory is what we lack

You can arrange your numbers to behave in any manner of ways

Nearly half of all of the carbon dioxide that humans have expelled

has fallen to the sea

Corrosive, corrosive the newly corrosive

Why was this buried?

Gray looks at her stained face thrown up in bewilderment.

Why, when what could have been protected—?

In order to protect something, a person must first, he pauses.

There is no comprehension in her face

How must he tell her and add another blow to this seemingly unscathed consciousness

In order to protect something, a person must first see—it is worth protecting

She turns, in disbelief
As he foresaw, this she could not fathom
Dearly matters, how can a person not see?
We thought it was ours, unerringly, for all time
Is there such a thing, as all time?
In a human existence, how long is that?
Needs burying, bullying. Thinking thoughts into submission

What form was she, he thought, to speak outside of language?

Remembering herself, she rises, says, *Forgive these truths*

She flings the documents about, *They must be known.*

Busy Intersections
of Anti-Matter

Bea reads this on the way, by her way she is on the way. She is holding the thought in front of her face as she is about to step out into traffic.

Things converge meaning to say is it the additional hidden after effects of global warming, now referred to as the rising warmth among us or RWAU effect, as if meaning to say that this represents some wonderful sign of affection.

The recurrent cry was all to the good. No one is accountable. Go and buy another high emissions producing vehicle for land, air or sea. Go find new non-renewable sources of fuel to your delight. As your delight is tantamount, is it not? Your delight. And think not of the delight of generations to come. They will inherit your appetites as well as your well -being and alacrity and there is always a way. The sky and sea and your powers of navigating are infinite and in-destructible.

Everyone is asking, What is S-K-Y? What is O-C-E-A-N?

Is there a corner of mistrust?

Bea has left the office and again opened her news scan account. Is she listening through a wireless device or is she intuiting what once amounted to radio waves, or is she glancing at a hand held device with text in code? Is she touching it in colored waves along a surface?

No matter, it was as if she held in front of her face the ancient device known as a newspaper, screening her view on every side. It was as if. And she did not look and she did not see what was in front of her.

Or was it as if, time stood still while many considered this matter. Do not step out into busy intersections of anti-matter while considering some disaster or other, some dishonest disclosure which has been held back and is only now appearing. Do not be so startled so as to take a step blindly.

And along the same deceptive path leading to the same eventual goal, do not be so ecstatic that you step out forgetting to survey traffic patterns. Be not so un-kind as to forget your neighbor.

Consider your neighbor, thought Gray. And he knew in that instant it was time to set out toward home. Was there a reason?

Not unlike an undeniable urge to create carbon emissions, to water one's lawn to default, to implicate enormous decorative fountains in a region of drought. Dare he say doubt, while speeding along toward the heavily trafficked intersection.

Intersection, do you dream of prosecution? Do you dream of being implicated in a waltz, a scene of civic disobedience? Do you visit with your many visitors in an ecstatic hope to be done with vessels being dropped into your gutters? Who has been lost along your borders and torn among your slabs of stone? Hanging one's head is a missive. None despite. Is this the breadth and the length of what has become?

A book is a thing which becomes us, or which may be hurled into oblivion. The other captivity.

Gray

When you look at a riveting stranger, you rarely think the picture is not complete. Before you have time to admire the perfectly sealed symmetry of a face, words might be spoken which break the image in parts which aren't actual.

Thus, in thought, Gray walked along the sidewalk.

He saw a figure walk out of a storefront, a figure indeed whose bones were nearly to be seen stridently carrying the form. The form of what? When you look at a riveting stranger you rarely think the picture is not complete. And yet. This picture was not. The form is, upon first glance not weak nor is it powerful. The figure is strong in intent. This should have been invisible, but it was not invisible to Gray. He watched her walking perhaps with too much intent to reach somewhere. Where was she going? She did not look out into the street before crossing.

Bea

Of what luxuries does she dream? Of sleep. She dreams of the restful sleep of youth where one may wearily lay down one's head with literally no worries. Or if there are worries they are for oneself and not one's children. One's own worries may be sublimated in ways worries for one's child may never be shunted. At least, this was not possible for Bea.

She sat at the little desk, perplexed at what garments to stretch across this sheathe of non-reality. Was she heard or not heard?

The mechanical face of the interviewer which watched could only be described this way because to Bea it was unfamiliar. But the geometric glasses, and the youth of the face made it seem all too sure and simultaneously not sure at all, as if her poise were an accessory which wouldn't last. But it looked so lovely in the light and Bea wished she could possess a little bit of it. Even a tinge of frost along the line of her untelling lip. The catastrophic ankles held easily in pin up shoes which crossed themselves as if to say, *I can certainly manage this apparatus*. But what part of her was not apparatus? The speaking part seemed to say, "see me." And the non-speaking parts seemed all to scheme in order that they be seen separately. Was she competing with someone? Bea wasn't the sort to compete. She was more the sort to compete with her non-shadow. She was the sort to compete with the depths of nothingness. But her interviewer of course couldn't know this. And clearly, her interviewer was in competition with herself more so than anyone else. Her interviewer didn't know this either. Neither did Bea, who had been hoping for the warmth one never receives on such occasions. Still, she had been hoping for it, since no one had ever taught her not to hope. And she herself wasn't capable of existing any other way. She did not even entertain the possibility of not hoping. It would be the same as not breathing. It wasn't possible. Persons didn't exist that way, or so she thought.

Bea did know that the momentary blindness of first meetings had to be dealt with carefully. She maintained a particular fondness for this blindness, where someone can become anyone. She enjoyed watching persons invent themselves and wondered if she would ever be able to do so herself.

She left the office, clutching an employment listing. Grateful for the possibility of anything else. Something beyond the Department of Veneer Illustration. It was a chance. Regardless of the unlikelihood of her getting the job, she left the employment office sheerly elated.

As she stepped off of the curb there appeared abruptly a yellow SUV, larger than life with which she was about to collide, whereupon a fair-haired foreigner rapidly grasped her by the shoulders and pulled her back. What she saw was the color of the hour, which appeared to be ivory. This was blinding at first, the sense of time being color as she felt her legs beneath her somewhat unsteadily.

She barely comprehended what had occurred when she began to shake uncontrollably. The foreigner supported her and guided her to a nearby bench. He asked her several questions, but for many moments she could not speak. She was seeing, and could not relate to this person, or to anyone for that matter. She thought, *invisible light with one-thousand pointed rays.* Things appeared brighter, louder. As if her senses had stepped outside of her body to bring the stimulus nearer, more violently so.

And then her vision was just starting to clear, and she heard him saying something about an ambulance. She could hear the odd tones of his cell phone as he awkwardly, though definitely, began to call—. And here she interrupted him.

—As for the future.

He stopped dialing and looked into her face in an odd way she could not have described. But then her expression began to open until she had fully returned to the bench and the stranger and she began to speak as if she had been speaking all along.

—No, thank you, I won't need a doctor. I'm not hurt and I must—. What is your name?

—Gray.

—Thank you, Gray, for the future. And I was just going—.

—What is your name?—He was more than a little unsettled and there was something about her face in particular which he could not name, which compelled him to ask.

—Bea.

—Bea?

—Yes, well short for Macabea, and—studying him, now fully alert to her circumstances.—Gray?

— Please, let me walk with you.

SPUYTEN DUYVIL

Meeting Eyes Bindery
Triton
Lithic Scatter

Made in the USA
Charleston, SC
07 January 2013